PLAGUE OF GULLS

STEPHEN GREGORY was born in Derby, England and earned a degree in law from the University of London. His first novel, *The Cormorant* (1986), won Britain's prestigious Somerset Maugham Award and drew comparisons to Poe. The book was also adapted for film as a BBC production starring Ralph Fiennes. Two more novels, both set in Wales, followed: *The Woodwitch* (1988) and *The Blood of Angels* (1994).

After a year working with director William Friedkin (*The Exorcist*) as a screenwriter in Hollywood, Stephen spent fifteen years teaching in Borneo, and during the long, hot tropical evenings he wrote four more novels, set back home in rural England and Wales. He now lives in France with his wife Chris, in a small house beside the river Vienne, where they're slowly rebuilding a 16th-century fortified farmhouse. Six of his novels and one story collection are available from Valancourt.

By Stephen Gregory

The Cormorant (1986)*

The Woodwitch (1988)*

The Blood of Angels (1994)*

The Perils and Dangers of this Night (2008)

The Waking That Kills (2013)*

Wakening the Crow (2014)*

Plague of Gulls (2015)*

On Dark Wings: Stories (2019)*

* Published by Valancourt Books

PLAGUE OF GULLS

STEPHEN GREGORY

VALANCOURT BOOKS

Plague of Gulls by Stephen Gregory
Originally published digitally in serial format by Pigeonhole in 2015
First published in book form by P. S. Publishing in 2018
First edition Valancourt Books edition 2021

Published by Valancourt Books, Richmond, Virginia
http://www.valancourtbooks.com

ISBN 978-1-954321-10-6 (*hardcover*)
ISBN 978-1-948405-97-3 (*trade paperback*)

Also available as an electronic book.

Cover illustration by Sandra Gómez
Cover design by Mauricio Villamayor

Set in Dante MT

November in Snowdonia. I'm in the caravan up at the quarry.

The gulls are going crazy, screaming and battering at the windows with their wings. I can hear the slither of their feet on the roof as they land and take off again.

When I open the door, step outside and fling them a handful of bread and biscuit, they fight and gobble as though they're starving and then they beat away from me, a white and black and grey cloud. I shut the door and walk to the edge of the quarry.

It's cold, eight o'clock in the morning. There's a silvery drizzle blowing in the air.

My stump's hurting. The doctor said it'll ache when the winter comes. He said I'll feel the ghost of the missing finger when the days get colder. The ghost is haunting me already, a throbbing pain where the finger used to be. I cup both hands around my mug of tea and peer over the brink of the quarry.

My quarry. It still seems strange. It belongs to me, the hole, and everything in it. The gulls, all mine.

The birds calm down once they've woken me and winkled me out of the caravan. And the pain in my hand eases a bit as I press it to the hot mug. Standing on the edge, I look down into the pool, a hundred feet below me. The water's always different. It changes with the time of day and the light on the surface. In the mornings, before the sun's risen over the hillside, it's perfectly black, perfectly smooth, and I can see deeply into it.

Dad's car. I can make out the humped, rounded shape of it, lying in the pool like a dead whale. Dimly, the headlamps peer up at me.

Shivering. Hard to believe, not so long ago it was August, the summer, the carnival in town. November ... the word sends a shiver down my spine.

I blink away from the round eyes at the bottom of the pool and look about the quarry. It's littered with the rubbish which people bring up from Caernarfon: there's a raggedy kind of avalanche, where people have driven up and slung their bags and boxes and broken machinery, unwanted bits of their homes, their gardens, their lives. A spillage of discarded stuff, snagged on the rocks on its way down to the pool ...

A strange inheritance. I own a hole a hundred feet deep, and all the air and water in it. I own all the broken, unnecessary things which are thrown into it. And hundreds of gulls, which come to the quarry for the pickings and to wake me in the morning for their breakfast.

My tea's going cold. I sling the dregs onto the ground. I look up to the top of the hill, the iron fence and rusted barbed wire which are supposed to stop sheep and curious hikers from coming too close. Down to the town, miles below me: the gleam of slate from the rooftops, the towers of the castle no more than a glimmer of grey through the drizzle.

Cold. I turn away from the quarry, with just a glance at the pool again. A flurry of a breeze picks up a sheet of newspaper. It whirls in the air, folding and turning this way and that, and a few of the gulls dive to the hole, as though they think the flutter of white is a gull from another quarry trespassing on their territory. But then they twist away, and the paper settles on the water. It spreads and darkens and sinks. The outline of the car blurs and disappears.

I turn back to the caravan. When I open the door, there's a rush of air and some of the gulls drop to the roof and land there. They try to get into the door as I squeeze inside. For a mad moment, there's a brawling of wings and their big rubbery feet and jabbing beaks around my shoulders as they try to force themselves past me ...

'No, not you! And not you! And not you!'

I yell at them, and I beat them off with my hands. They clack on my mug with their horny beaks. And then, when they fall away from me, squalling among themselves, one of them springs forward again . . .

'Yes, you! Get inside!'

I let the bird come in, between my legs and into the caravan, and I quickly shut the door.

Outside, the racket gets louder and louder. All the gulls in the quarry are banging at the windows and on the roof to try and get in. I pull the curtains shut and sit on the bed, with my hands around the cooling mug. Minute by minute, the commotion subsides, until my little space and the world outside are quiet again.

'You,' I say to the bird. 'This is all because of you.' Right now, it's standing on the end of my bed, rearranging a few ruffled feathers with the tip of its beak. At the sound of my voice, it cocks its head to one side and looks at me with a bright black eye. 'Yes, you. What makes you think you're so different from all the others?'

And you? the bird seems to say to me. What's so special about you?

Nothing special. No claim to fame. I'm David Kewish, eighteen years old. Five years in a dingy little private school in Bangor and then I do so badly in my exams that not a university in the land will take me in.

David Kewish, sitting in a caravan in a Welsh quarry, with my gull. It pants into my face. I love that smell. The carpet feels damp, and the rumpled bed I've been sleeping on. I see myself in the wardrobe mirror. Funny—even when I'm tousled and bleary I look all right, a well-made teenage boy with a clear complexion and thick black hair. Nothing special.

It was a strange summer. Some upsetting things happened. That's why I've come up to the quarry, to let it all blow over. Rumours and whispers and tales about me. About the bird. About me and the bird.

A strange summer. People got hurt. Was it one or two? Or three? Who's counting?

ONE

The finger? It happens on 5th May, on my birthday.

I've got myself a guitar. I had one before, which Mum and Dad bought me for passing my O levels. I loved it, and the companionship it gave me with my best friends at school: a summer on the beach, cosy autumn evenings and wintry afternoons, hours and days of strumming and finger-picking and bending the strings and thinking we were pretty good at it. But then Dad got ill—he knew he was ill and didn't do much about it—and he died. And the music seemed to curl up and wither and die like Dad had done. Now, a couple of years later, I'm thinking I'll take up the guitar again and decide to treat myself for my birthday.

Another reason ... to spite Kenny. Mum calls him my stepfather. She took up with him not long after Dad had gone. Kenny Phelps. He isn't working, he's never worked, he can't and won't buy me a present, so I know it'll piss him off if I buy something for myself.

Especially a guitar. Kenny's an air guitarist. He can't play a note on a real guitar, but he's got a reputation in town as an air guitarist. In pubs, at parties, people ask him to play. They clear a space for him and applaud his every move, his every sway and grimace as he bends his imaginary strings, does his note-perfect renditions of those endless, cheesy, fossilized guitar solos from the sixties and seventies and eighties.

My birthday, I come down to the living room with my carefully wrapped, guitar-shaped parcel.

Kenny's hunched on the sofa, nursing a mug of coffee in both hands. He was out drinking last night. He doesn't

8

say anything, but he glances up as I sit in the armchair on the other side of the room. He reeks of booze. He hasn't shaved or even splashed his face. Scrubbed up, he can be quite good-looking, almost a skinny middle-aged rock star in denims and cowboy boots . . . but hung over, in the beery Black Sabbath T-shirt he's been sleeping in, his hair long and lank and grey, he's beady and beaky like a crow. Bulging black underpants. Bare, hairy legs. His hands shake as he lifts the coffee to his mouth. His lips recoil from the heat and his teeth make a little quivery snarl.

He's put out. Good. He manages a yellowy smile, but I can tell he's put out, as I open a birthday card I've written to myself, as I read it and chuckle as though I've never seen it before and then stand it on top of the television. 'Happy 18th,' it says on the front in big silver letters. And then I unwrap the parcel. Kenny watches, the smile like a wound on his mouth.

The guitar case is soft black imitation leather. I unzip it. It's lined with silver nylon fur. I slide the guitar out and nestle it onto my knee.

An acoustic guitar with lightweight steel strings: not expensive, but perfect for relearning and practising the chords I've almost forgotten. I feel the urge to try it straightaway, a warm wash of feeling right through my body, that the guitar'll be the key to a long, hot, happy summer, rekindling friendships, making new friends. My left hand goes to the frets, my fingers form an easy E major. I lift my right hand to strum my very first chord on the present I've bought myself—but then I stop and glance at Kenny to enjoy the expression on his face.

'Oh sorry, Kenny.' I can't resist the temptation to niggle him a bit more. 'D'you want to have a go? Maybe you could tune it for me?'

He winces. 'All right maestro, all right. Actually I didn't forget your birthday.' He leans creakily backwards on the

sofa and feels for something under one of the cushions. 'I
peeked into your room and saw the guitar all wrapped up,
and so I got you a tiny something to go with it . . .'

He tosses it across the room, and I catch it: a rolled-up
tube of paper, maybe a calendar wrapped in cheap birthday paper. 'Go on, open it,' he says.

It's a laminated photograph, scrolled up tightly with
elastic bands, which I unroll onto my knee. The legendary
Jimi Hendrix . . . kneeling on stage at some long-ago concert, his guitar a blaze of golden flames. The guitar's bent
and broken, he must've smashed it already as part of his
act, and now he's kneeling in front of it, all reverent and
aghast, as though he's cremating the body of a best friend
or relative.

'The Monterey festival, 1967,' Kenny says. 'Inspiration
for you. You never know when you'll need it.'

I look at the photo, frown and manage to readjust my
face into a smile. 'Inspiration, yeah thanks,' I murmur, not
sure how inspiring it is to see someone burning his guitar
when I've just bought myself a new one. 'Hendrix was
great. I'll stick him on the wall.'

I roll up the photo. The stiff plastic lamination makes it
want to spring open, so I snap the elastic bands around it
again.

He grins crookedly at me, and I can see, through the
fustiness of his hangover, the twinkle in his eyes, which is
part of his small-town charisma, the glimmer of mischie-
vous charm he uses to create his tiny bit of local celebrity.
I don't hate him. I don't really dislike him. So I suddenly
feel mean and clumsy, with the guitar on my knee and my
birthday card on the television.

'Look,' he goes on, 'I know you're landed gentry and
I'm just one of the great unwashed, but would you do
something for me? I'm wrecked and I need a cigarette. Can
you run across the street and get some for me? I promise

I'll keep an eye on your precious guitar. It'll still be here when you get back . . .'

Exasperated, but oddly relieved to get out of the room, I stand up and lean the guitar onto the armchair. Kenny gropes for a scatter of loose change by the phone and hands me a few coins. I hurry downstairs and pull open the front door. I'm out in the street, about to cross over to the pub, when I hear Kenny calling something else . . . So I stop and turn and try to catch what he's saying. For a split second I put my hand up to the door as I strain to hear him.

He comes tumbling down the narrow staircase. 'And a lighter, hey Dave, get me a lighter, will you?' At the foot of the stairs he trips and stumbles towards me. With a cheery 'Oops!' he puts out his hands to break his fall, hits the front door, and bangs it shut.

It's a heavy wooden door with thick heavy panes of glass in it. My left forefinger's inside the hinge.

I hardly feel it at first. Just the crash of the door and the crunch of gristle and bone as I jump backwards into the street.

I remember staring, amazed, at the pumping of blood. It splatters onto the cobbles. And then the pain . . . a jolt of it through my arm and into my shoulder and neck and right into the top of my skull.

The rest of the day falls bitterly into place.

It could almost be funny, the stupid irony of it all, and because the injury itself mightn't seem so terrible. I mean, I'm not going to die or anything. The landlord from the pub sees it happen. He and one of his girls bind my hand with a table napkin, to try and stop the bleeding and to stop me from staring at it and moaning. Kenny's flapping about, ridiculous in his T-shirt and pants, his bare feet smeared with blood. All he can do, as the landlord gets us into his car and we set off to the hospital, is wave a soggy red envelope at me as I sit whimpering on the back seat and say, 'Hey Dave, I found this, I found this, they might be able to do something with this . . .'

He's spotted a piece of my finger, crushed into the hinge of the door and left behind as I stepped away from the impact. He's teased it out and plopped it into an envelope.

They take me to the hospital, and with a couple of pricks of a hypodermic needle all the pain's gone. No, the doctor says, appraising the mash of gristle and bone that Kenny's brought with him . . . the severed remains are no good for anything. He'll just tidy up the finger and stitch it as neatly as he can and I'll live the rest of my life with an unfortunate, negligible disability. The doctor makes a joke, knowing I'm feeling no pain just then and assuming, wrongly, that I'm enjoying my role as a wounded soldier . . . 'You won't miss it at all, young man,' he says, 'except maybe when you go swimming and you find yourself going round and round in one big circle.'

Ha ha. I have a big, fat, white bandage where my fore-finger used to be.

As Kenny predicted, the guitar's still there when I get back to the house. It's glowing in the afternoon sunshine, lovely, curvaceous, tempting. I just stare at it, and then I carry it upstairs, with the case, and prop it into the corner of my room. Somehow, I don't want to put it back in the case, zipped up like a corpse in a body bag.

The same evening, my finger starts hurting. The anaesthetic wears off. Throbbing . . . slow and steady, a rhythm of blood, the pulse of my pain.

I stay upstairs, my arm in a sling, the bandage bulging as though the remains of my finger are mummified inside it. Kenny's downstairs, in the street outside the door. I can hear his voice and I know that the landlord's come over to talk to him and bring him a beer. I hear the *whoosh-whoosh-*

whoosh of the brush as he scrubs at the blood on the cobbles. And I guess he's slopping out the hinge of the door with warm soapy water.

Happy 18th birthday. And then, through days and nights of a dull pounding pain, I stare at my guitar, at its shapely body and the silent black hole in its belly.

A fortnight, and then the bird comes to me. It takes off the bandage and it's time to have a look at the finger.

TWO

The bird? It comes on the night of 21st May.

The pain's woken me. No, I've hardly been sleeping. The throbbing's kept me half-awake, tossing and wriggling through a muddle of thoughts and confusing images since I came to bed at midnight.

Tugging at my rumpled sheets, I bang the bandage on the bedhead. A dazzling pain, through my hand and my wrist and into my arm and my shoulder.

I grit my teeth. I fold my hand into my armpit and squeeze it, to try and ease the throb throb throb, to slow the beating of the blood. I roll onto my side and glare across the room, into the darkness of a troubled night.

The guitar's leaning in the corner. As my eyes adjust to the shadows, the shape of it seems to bulge and swell, and the black hole in the middle of its body is like a mouth. An open mouth, empty and soundless, just gaping at me.

Silence. It doesn't sigh or moan or even breathe. It's a dead mouth, in a dead guitar.

And then there's a sound in the silence. I listen hard and hear a gentle tapping. Not in the room. It's from outside, from somewhere along the town wall, near the open skylight above my bed. No, it's coming from the street, below the window on the other side of the room. It stops and starts, an irregular, insistent tapping, as though someone's out there and knocking idly on the front door with a coin or a pebble or a key . . .

So I get out of bed and move across the room, still with my left hand in my right armpit. The window's already open. I lean out and look down.

No one. The street's deserted. Twll Yn Yr Wal, that's what it's called, the hole in the wall. An orange lamp is flickering, so that the cobbles gleam and glisten and strange shadows play on the ivy-covered walls of the old town. To my left, the towers of the castle are square black blocks. To my right, the narrow medieval street is a tunnel, burrowing into darkness. A hole.

The church bell strikes one, a metallic jarring note. The tapping continues, right below me, and I lean further out of the window.

'Who's there?' I whisper.

I go as softly as I can down the stairs. Kenny's door is ajar and he's snoring. I catch a waft of alcohol and pull his door shut. Down through the living room on the first floor, where the dog's asleep on the sofa. Down again, to the ground floor—from top to bottom of a little three-storey terraced townhouse.

The tapping's louder. No beat, no rhythm, only the mystery of a coded message I can't decipher. I open the door and step outside.

A sudden shuffling and flapping . . . and before I can see what it is or try to stop it, a black shape rustles past my feet and into the house. A piece of shadow . . . it undoes itself from the cobbles and flutters through the door, as though it's been waiting for me to come downstairs and let it in.

A bird. It's been tapping on the bottom of the door with its beak.

'Hey,' I hiss at it. 'You'd better get out . . .'

It's a gull, only a few weeks old but already bulky and

strong, probably gorged on chips and crisps and bits of bread which the tourists have been throwing to it. It cocks its head sideways and angles a round black eye up at me.

May. There are gulls nesting on the rooftops all over town. This is the time when the chicks begin to slither down the slates, fall off, and flutter to the pavements . . . lots of them, waddling through the crowds of holidaymakers, in and out of the traffic, mewing and squeaking like so many fat brown chickens. This one looks up at me for a moment—I see a strange silvery gleam on its beak—and then it leans across to peck inquisitively at my bare foot.

'No you don't . . . Let's get you out . . .'

I try to manoeuvre past it and force it back into the street, but it unfolds its wings and beats away from me, towards the foot of the stairs. I release my hand from my armpit and lean closer to the bird to shoo it out.

Two things happen at once. The sudden movement makes the blood start pounding in my wounded finger, so loud in my head that it seems as though the bird itself can hear it . . . and at the same moment, the gull springs at me and jabs at the bandage. I gasp at the pain and recoil, and the bandage snags on its beak. The whole of it, a big tube of gauze, comes off my finger.

The gull leaps away from me. With the bandage stuck on its beak, it disappears up the stairs.

I quickly close the front door. Just in time. There's a yelp from the living room overhead, and the dog comes tumbling down. Quivering with shock and fear, she presses her body against my legs and stares at the foot of the stairs, terrified in case the extraordinary creature that's come flapping into her life and woken her up might reappear at any moment.

'It's all right, it's all right.' I pick her up with my right hand. I hold my left hand behind my back. I don't want to see my finger. It's the first time the bandage has come off.

For the first time since the accident, I feel the nakedness of it, the cool air on it, and I wonder what it might look like.

'Don't worry, the big bird won't hurt you. It's just a baby, like you. I'll make it go up into my room and out of the window. I won't let it hurt you . . .'

Sure enough, by the time I reach the first floor and drop the dog back onto the sofa, there's no sign of the gull. I look around all the furniture and behind the television, shuffling my feet and making shooing noises, and then I continue up and up to the top of the house, past Kenny's room and towards my own. I can feel the shiver of the air on my bare finger, and the throb of it. I don't want to see it. Not yet. I'll get the bird out of the house, find the tube of the bandage, and slip it back where it's come from, without looking to see what the finger's like.

That's the plan. When I step into my bedroom and close the door behind me, the gull's standing on the sill of the open window. A strange otherworldly sight . . . it seems bigger and more menacing, framed in the space, lit by the orange flicker of the streetlamp. The bandage has unravelled into one long strip of bloodstained material, and the bird's shaking it from side to side, trying to unsnag the length of white gauze from its beak as it whirls and whips and catches the breeze from the street outside.

Only a bird, but a bullying presence in my room. A wild creature, with a gleam in its eyes, flicking the bandage at me as though daring me to come and get it.

I hesitate. Still with my left hand behind my back, I step forward, meaning the gull to flop out of the window, go spiralling down and down to the cobbles below.

But it leaps straight at me. I step aside and wave at it in mid-air with both of my hands. It batters at its own reflection in the wardrobe mirror. Thrashing its wings, it tries for a few moments with all its strength to reach the skylight in the ceiling of the room, scrabbling with its slappy webbed feet at the frame of the little window. The bandage trails from its beak. And then it flutters down and crash lands onto the guitar case on the floor. Panting, exhausted, it shuffles its wings and settles there, quite oblivious of me as I stand and stare and watch it.

The dead hours of a dark night. I sit on the end of my bed. I squeeze my eyes tight shut and blow softly onto my wounded finger, to try and slow down the throbbing. For a moment I'm tempted to peek through the narrowest of slits to see what the damage is like. But I don't.

I wait for the pain to ease. The walls of the castle and the old town lean around the house and smother it with their shadows.

When I open my eyes, the gull's still sitting on the guitar case. The streetlamp blinks on and off. I catch a silvery gleam from the bird's beak and lean closer to see what it is.

'Sssh ...' The gull angles its head towards me, as though mesmerised by the size of the big black shape which is leaning over it. 'Let me see.'

The bird has an aluminium ring-pull from a tin of beer stuck on its beak. It must've been pecking at it, searching around the rubbish bins for crisps and chips and thrown-away sandwiches, and somehow pushed the two tips of its beak through the two holes in the ring-pull. The beak's fastened tightly shut.

'That'll have to come off, or you'll die of starvation.' I lean even nearer, and the bird stays still, breathing hard through its nostrils. 'Good job you stuffed yourself full of food before you got this thing stuck on you. It's got to come off, or you won't last long out there ...'

No drama. No manic flapping. No whirl of feathers, no squirts of droppings.

First of all I light a candle, one of the scented candles I

need to light whenever I come back from the quarry. The bird stares at the flame, sneezes at the puther of smoke, transfixed by the quiver of the light and the odd perfume. I take a sheet from my bed, spin it lightly in the air and let it billow softly down . . . and the bird, maybe thinking that the gathering darkness is just another nightfall, doesn't try to avoid it.

With my right hand I feel under the sheet. The bird's quite still in the folds of its cave. My fingers find its breast and the beat of a quickly pumping heart. Its body is hot. But the beak is cold and hard, a curiously shaped bone, and I can feel how the curved tips of it have gone through the holes in the aluminium and got stuck there.

Easy. I gently waggle the ring-pull this way and that, until it slips off the beak.

'Got it. Is that why you came to see me?'

I lift the sheet off the bird. It swivels its head round and up to follow the movement, as though a great cloud has blown away and left the sky clear again. Sensing straight-away that the ring has gone, it opens and closes its beak, clacking the jaws together, and then it yawns a long and marvellous yawn to flex the muscles which have been cramped for as long as the ring's been there. I catch the smell of its breath. The smell of the beach, the sea, the smell of the night. Lit by the fluttering candle, the inside of its mouth is pink. It has a long, sharp tongue, like the blade of a scalpel.

'Look.' I show it the ring-pull. The bird tries to snatch it from my fingers. Dodging the jab of the beak, I say, 'Hey stupid, I just got it off you. I'm showing you so you'll remember to leave them alone from now on. If you get another one stuck on your beak, you've had it. Under-stand?'

But the bird seems drawn to the ring of metal which would've starved it to death if I'd left it there. I move it backwards and forwards in front of its eyes, intrigued by the way the gull follows it, like a cobra mesmerised by the swaying of a snake charmer's flute. Without thinking, as though I'm under the same spell I've cast on the bird, I transfer the ring to my left hand and hold it closer to the flame of the candle. And so, for the first time, I catch a glimpse of the place where my left forefinger used to be.

Only a glimpse. A split-second vision of a knobby stump and a crusted scab.

Because the bird lunges at the ring, or my finger. With a single beat of its powerful wings, it's on the bed and jabbing and jabbing, either at the lure of the candlelit ring or the swollen redness of my wound. Once, twice, three times, before I can sweep the maddened creature off the bed and onto the floor, it strikes the ring, knocking it from my hand and somewhere into the rumpled bedclothes. The beak bangs onto the finger. The pain floods my brain.

Hissing and spluttering, 'Get out! Get out!' I jump to my feet and drive the bird across the room, whirling at it with my arms. At last it springs to the window and flings itself outside.

Gone. 'Ungrateful bloody thing ...' I'm muttering through clenched teeth. I lean over and see the bird spinning out of control to the cobbles below my window. It manages to angle its clumsy fledgling wings enough to parachute down and soften its fall, landing with a slap of its webbed feet and a clatter of its beak onto the ground. A ragged heap of brown feathers. 'Piss off, will you ...'

Gone. I stare down and try to see where it'll go, so angry that I just want to make sure it's hopped up the street and away. I want to see it go. But it just vanishes. As the lamplight flickers infuriatingly on and off, the bird disappears in the same way it appeared. It becomes a piece of shadow. It folds into the black shadows of the sleeping town.

The street is still and silent and empty. No one. No bird.

I go back to my bed, sit on it, and blow out the candle. The room seems darker than ever, now that the flame is out. I can barely make out the shape of the guitar leaning in the corner, the black hole in its belly. The unravelled bandage is just a pale scribbling on the floor. The plume of perfumed smoke becomes a part of the darkness.

I had a glimpse of my finger. Ugly. I don't want to see it again, not now. So I lie on my side, curled into a ball, with my left hand nestled between my thighs, and the pain ebbs and ebbs . . . until I think I might close my eyes and sleep.

THREE

Sunday morning. The smell of coffee and bacon from downstairs. Kenny's making breakfast.

As always, every morning the first thing I see when I open my eyes is the guitar . . . and as always, it reminds me straightaway of what happened to my finger. So I feel with my right hand to make sure that the bandage is still in place.

Nothing. When I gingerly touch my left wrist and left hand and feel for the familiar fat soft tubing of the bandage, there's nothing. I touch a raw, naked place where my forefinger's been injured.

I quickly glance down from my pillow, without raising my head. My eyes follow the long strip of white and blood-stained ribbon across the floor. At the other end of it, the gull is snuggled comfortably on my guitar case, nibbling at the bandage with its heavy grey beak.

'Hey, you. What d'you think you're doing? How the hell did you get back in?'

The gull stares at me from the comfort of the guitar case. It's nudging the gauze around its plump body and wide webbed feet, as though rearranging the materials of its nest. In answer to my second question, it cocks one eye to the overhead skylight, where a few downy brown feathers are stuck to the frame. During the night, the bird must've found itself on top of the ivy-covered walls of the old town and hopped onto the roof of our house, which butts right against them. For some reason—or for no reason—it's tumbled through the skylight and back into my room. And for a weird second, I have a feeling that I'm glad it's here.

Deep in the darkness of my bed, I touch the tip of my finger. The gull watches me. The guitar watches me.

I close the gull inside my room, leaving the skylight wide open so it can flutter up and onto the roof if it wants to, and I go downstairs.

On my way through the living room I pick up Pumpkin in the crook of my right arm. She's been asleep on the sofa, lying flat on her back with her head thrown back, her mouth open and legs splayed. She's about six months old, special to me because I found her and rescued her from the castle ditch: a dark afternoon at the end of last October, I hear a commotion of jackdaws down in the moat and I slither down to see what's happening. When the birds whirl away, I find this tiniest puppy, only a week old, which must've tumbled down or been thrown down there by some stupid kids. In fact, before I can even bend to take a closer look, a gobby little moron from the council estate, with a thin pale face and spikey red hair, is pelting me with gravel from some nearby roadworks ... The jackdaws squawk and flap around my head, the kid runs off, and I scramble out of the ditch with the puppy tucked into my jacket pocket. 'Pumpkin,' Kenny says straightaway when I bring her home. He's in the kitchen, a big knife in one hand, a handful of orange mush in the other, a hefty rum and coke within easy reach, hollowing a pumpkin for Halloween. So I clean her up in the kitchen sink, and as he's cutting out the fangs of the mask she waddles across the draining board and bites Kenny as hard as she can with her needle-sharp teeth . . . to show him that her fangs are sharper than the mask's.

'Ah, it's the squire, Squire David Kewish,' he says now, Sunday morning, as I go into the kitchen. He looks and smells unusually well—showered and shaved, splashed with cologne, although his hands are shaking as always. He's made bacon sandwiches and coffee for both of us. 'Good day to you, and'—he ruffles the puppy's head as I put her onto the floor—'and good morning, Pumpkin.'

'Hey Kenny,' I say, 'do you want to take a look at this?'

He can tell from the smallness of my voice that I've got something serious I need to share with him, that I'm not in the mood for his banter. He turns to me, wiping his hands on a dishcloth, and then he slings the cloth into the sink. He wipes his palms up and down his T-shirt. 'All right Dave, let's see, in the light, over here . . .'

He reaches for my left arm, which I'm still holding behind my back, firmly straightens it out and unfolds my hand close to the kitchen window.

We both appraise the finger. The last time I saw it, it was pumping blood onto the street outside our front door. Since then, despite the pulpy mess that Kenny brought with him in its gory envelope, I've imagined that the tip of the finger's been squashed and repaired and is somehow still there. But it's gone altogether. The whole of the top of the finger is missing. There's a big crusty scab of blood on the knob of the middle joint, with black nylon stitches prickling out of it, and nothing else.

Kenny's angling my hand this way and that, in and out of the sunshine which is falling through the window and gleaming on the sink and draining board. 'Not bad, not bad,' he's murmuring, 'nice job, nice job . . .' as though the repetition is reassuring, as though saying something twice will make it twice as right. I tug my hand away and hold the scabby stump close to my eyes.

It's horrible. A piece of me—a piece I counted on having and using in the immediate weeks and months of my life—is gone.

'Hey Dave,' Kenny's saying, trying to put his arm around my shoulders, 'at least it's out now, you can see it and start to think about how you're going to work around it. I'm sorry if you think it was my fault, but I'll try to help you as much as I can. Is it still hurting?'

We have our sandwiches together in the living room, eating from trays on our laps. Out of a habit I quickly got into since the accident, I eat with my right hand and hold the other hand out of sight. In fact the finger does feel better, out of the bandage. The air's cool on it, and it isn't throbbing at all. But I don't feel like talking. I try to eat, but the food seems to congeal into a paste in my throat. Kenny's telling me something about his 'work' from the previous afternoon and evening, mumbling through a mouthful of bread and bacon and wiping the tomato sauce from his lips with the back of his hand. I'm hardly listening. I watch him, and I feel a knot of dislike for him tightening in my stomach. I'm thinking about the guitar upstairs in my bedroom, leaning in the corner and waiting for me to come and try it. I'm remembering how I held it for less than a minute on the morning of my birthday, before Kenny, the celebrated air guitarist, asked me to run outside and get him some cigarettes.

I push a bit of bacon into my mouth and chew it until all the flavour's gone and it's only a wad of gristle. At the same time, with my left hand behind my back again, I shape my fingers into the chords I know, dismayed to remember that nearly all of them need my forefinger to make them complete. Not all of them, but nearly all.

I take out the piece of gristle. Pumpkin, waiting

patiently at my feet, nibbles it gently from the palm of my hand. 'I'm not hungry,' I say. 'I need some air. I'll get the bus up to the quarry.'

Kenny pulls a face and nods at me. He's looking at me in a sorry, quizzical kind of way, holding a crust of bread in mid-air as though he's been paralysed for a moment. His hand's trembling, his left hand, the well-manicured, perfectly intact fingers with which he so expertly caresses the frets of his air guitar. The sight of them, held up in the morning sunshine for me to admire, makes the knot in my stomach rise into my throat.

At last, he pops the bread into his mouth. At the same time, deliberately mangling the words like some kind of zombie to try to cheer me up, he says, 'No worries, squire, you don't want to mope around the house with a dead-leg like me. Hey, why don't you come on my tour this evening? I've got a group lined up . . .'

He swallows the toast with an exaggerated gulping of his Adam's apple. I carry my tray through to the kitchen. On a sudden impulse, prompted by the calling of the gulls around the walls of the town, I pick up the scraps of bacon and bits of rind from my plate, as well as the crusts I don't feel like eating, wrap them into a piece of tissue, and bring them out of the kitchen. As I head out of the living room and turn to go up to my room, Kenny sees what I've got in my hand. 'You'll spoil that dog,' he says, 'you'll make her into a fat little pumpkin . . .'

Sure enough, the puppy follows me upstairs. But at the top, I nudge her out of the way with my foot and let myself into my bedroom. I close her out, sit down on my bed, and unfold the scraps from the tissue.

FOUR

The bird takes the pieces of bacon very delicately from my fingers. It jiggles them between the heavy grey jaws of its beak, turning them this way and that before gulping them down, as though the pieces of meat are still alive . . . living creatures picked out of a rock pool on the beach or delivered by a parent bird.

A big fat baby. It seems bigger and sturdier than the other silly, wobbly bundles of brown feathers which are pattering around the town on their flat grey webbed feet. It puzzles at the crusts of toast, shaking them and dropping them and picking them up again, glancing around the room as if it's looking for a pool of water to soak them in and make them a bit easier to get down . . . They're too dry, something to discard, like the salty bits of a dried-up starfish or cuttlefish or some other inedible wreckage thrown up on the beach. The bird tries everything with the toast until, with an impatient toss of its head and a shiver of its mottled plumage, it throws the fragments over its shoulder.

I hear Pumpkin scratching at the bedroom door. She knows there's bacon and she's got an inkling that someone or something other than herself is devouring it.

I call out, too late, 'No, Kenny, hang on . . .' when I see the door handle turning. And then the door opens, and the puppy comes rollicking into the room with Kenny close behind.

It could be mayhem. I lunge for Pumpkin, thinking to stop her from either going for the gull and shaking it into a mess of dead, raggedy feathers or, on the other hand, being pecked in the eyes by the bristling, startled bird.

But I don't need to. There's a long moment of those comical double takes from a corny old movie. Pumpkin skids to a halt and stares aghast at the bird, and then she cocks her head at me before she turns and stares at the bird again. The gull stands up as big as it can make itself, opens and raises both wings in an instinctively threatening gesture, hisses at the puppy until its breath runs out and then angles its head at me.

The dog and the bird eye each other suspiciously. There's a long silence once the bristling and hissing are done. And Kenny, who's paused at the door and stopped in surprise at seeing the bird in my guitar case, says at last, 'Well, who's this?'

Pumpkin jumps onto my bed and snuggles against me, as much for the security of being close to me as for staking her prior claim on me as her human. The bird makes a big show of rearranging its plumage, poking and prodding with its beak into all kinds of secret places under its wings and under its belly, and then sits down in the guitar case with the strip of bandage tucked underneath it.

I open my bedside drawer and show Kenny the ring-pull. 'It had this stuck on its beak. It wouldn't have been able to eat or drink anything. I got it off.'

He chuckles, disparaging, sneering. 'Watch out it doesn't start thinking you're its mother. It'll bond with you and then you'll be lumbered with it for good.'

He sits next to me on the bed—me and him and the puppy side by side—and we look at the gull.

'You know what I think?' he says at last. 'He's a big boy, or she's a big girl, I'm not sure which. Only a few weeks old, a fledgling just tumbled out of its nest on one of the rooftops here in town . . . just flopped out of the nest and onto the slates and then skidded off the edge and down into the street. But it looks kind of . . . well, kind of big.'

I start to get an idea of where he's going with this rambling train of thought. The gull, mottled a beautiful patterning of browns and black—a speckling and striping and shading of all the possible browns to be found in the sands and weeds and driftwood on all the nearby beaches—has a paler, greyer belly than the herring-gull chicks which are common in town. Yes, it's bigger, and paler. In the weight of its beak and the dead-coldness of its eyes, it's different. It looks at me, and something in the empty blackness of its eyes makes me blink and want to flinch away.

Kenny's seen it too. He holds out his fingers to the bird, and it shudders horribly, cringing away as though it can't bear to be touched by him.

And then it cranes its head up to the open skylight, where the walls of the castle butt onto the wall of the house.

We all look, instinctively following the eyes of the gull. Me and Kenny and the dog. We see a shadow, a blur of black wings pass across the window ... a shadow which spills into my room for a split second and is gone again. And then another, a second bigger blacker shadow. For a moment, a pair of silent, threatening wings blocks all the sunshine outside.

'You know what I think?' Kenny says again. 'It's a blackback. The parents will come looking for him. You'd better watch out, that's what I think.'

FIVE

'Why do you always do the quotation-mark thing, whenever you say Kenny's *working*?' Simon says. He imitates me, using two fingers on each hand to make imaginary quotation marks in the air. 'Especially now, with your gory stump, it's pretty gross.'

Simon Reece has dropped by to see me. We've been loafing all afternoon in my bedroom, at the top of the house in Hole in the Wall Street, Caernarfon. At first he spends a while stroking a few chords on the guitar, not really playing but just tuning it and trying it out, and then he leans it back into its corner. I can tell he doesn't want to play it properly in front of me. He doesn't want to make me feel worse than I already do about the coincidence of the accident on my birthday. A mate from schooldays, Simon's a tall, gangly, spotty guy, with flopping greasy hair. He got better grades than I did, nothing brilliant, but enough to squeeze a place at Bangor University, doing geography or sociology or something like that.

Of course I've shown him the finger. He seems undecided about how to react to it.

'Gross,' he says, recoiling from the swollen stump and its blackened scab. And then, to try and cheer me up, 'But it's going to be kind of cool, you know, when it stops looking so gruesome and maybe you start to get used to it?' He sees how downcast I am, and we both glance towards the guitar. He tries again. 'Maybe one day we'll both be cool, when I get rid of my spots and your stump is just a "distinguishing feature" on your passport.'

'Kenny's *working*,' I say again, and do the quotation marks into thin air. I've been telling Simon that Mum took off in April, exasperated by Kenny's stubbornness and pigheadedness and fecklessness . . . words I heard her use in their rows before she grabbed her rucksack and walked out. She got fed up with his drinking in the evenings, and the novelty of his fame as an air guitarist wore off long ago, after a spate of Christmas and New Year parties. Bored and frustrated, realising that her training as a nurse is wasted on a boozy workshy boyfriend and a dopey son, she's gone to help out in a refugee camp in Ethiopia or Somalia or somewhere like that . . .

I say, 'Kenny's picked up a bit of part-time *work* as a tour guide in the castle. You know, American tourists and Australian backpackers, he takes them up and down the towers and along the battlements for a few pounds a day. He calls it work. At least it keeps him out of the pub for a few hours in the afternoons . . . and in the evenings too, he does what he calls his *ghost tour,* a load of bollocks really. I guess Mum must've liked him, at least she did until a few months ago, but he does my head in. Sometimes I feel as though I could bloody . . .'

I stop myself from finishing the sentence, remembering the teasing way that Brian, up at the caravan, warned me about my threat. In any case, it irks me that I can't wholly dislike Kenny. He is, from time to time, infuriatingly like-able. He isn't clever or great-looking, but the little bit of talent and charisma he's got he kind of shares around . . . He's got a spirit which he shares with other people. And he's been around for Mum—yes, and for me—after Dad died. Sometimes a pain, often a mess, he's moved into our life because we need him, and it's bewildering to imagine the void in the house if he hadn't come and filled it.

'I've seen him doing the air guitar,' Simon says. We wince at each other. We don't need to say what we think about it. He puts his right hand between his legs, grabs his crotch and makes a schoolboyish gesture. 'Hotel Califor-nia . . .' He rubs at the air between his thighs . . . 'Bohemian Rhapsody . . . Sultans of Swing . . .' and he rubs faster and faster until he fakes a moaning orgasm.

I'm laughing . . . but then Simon does a strange thing, as though he's read my thoughts and he's agreeing with what I've just been thinking. He holds up a hand to stop me laughing. Imitating me by punctuating his quotation marks with his fingers, he says, 'Kenny Phelps is all right. He's a *character,* and a town like this needs characters. Yes, he's a piss-artist and a bullshitter . . . He calls himself a *local historian* because he knows a few stories about the castle, an *artist* because he's got a painting for sale in a tea-shop in Pool Street, a *journalist* because he had a letter published in the *Herald*. But he's all right. He niggles you because he's on your territory, because he's taken the place of your dad.'

For a moment I'm blank. And I'm stung, because he's right. A piss-artist? I know something about Kenny I thought I'd never tell anyone, an unpleasant little secret my mum shared with me.

I take a breath, think hard about the words I hear myself forming in my head. And then I say very quietly, 'Territory? You know what he does? He pisses in the wardrobe. Mum's told me, he's done it twice or three times. He rolls out of bed in the middle of the night and he pisses into her wardrobe, all over her clothes, all over my dad's clothes. She tries to stop him, but he's so drunk or sleepwalking or whatever, he doesn't know what he's doing and he shoves her away. And then he staggers back to bed again. In the morning he can't remember a thing. He just denies it and won't listen, even when she shows him the mess and the stink he's made.'

I pause. My voice is calm, but my hands are shaking. 'Territory . . . yes, that's it. He's marking his territory, like a dog pissing on a lamp post.'

Simon decides it's time to go home. I go down to the front door with him. We're cool. We haven't had a row or anything. In fact, I ask him if he wants to borrow the guitar, to take it home with him and play it—it's no good to me and he might as well enjoy it, if he wants to. He says no thanks. I watch him go mooching along Hole in the Wall Street, expecting him to turn and wave before he reaches the corner. He doesn't.

SIX

I go back upstairs. Pumpkin's asleep on the sofa. I pause at the door of Mum's bedroom and look inside. Kenny's clothes are all over the floor and the unmade bed. There's a strong smell of his sweat and the alcohol he's sweated into the sheets. I pick my way through and open the window. Immediately, a sweet cool breeze blows in, from the sea, from the beaches, through the dense green ivy which grows along the old town walls.

I continue up and up to the top of the house, to my own room. I can smell Simon, or rather the smell of whatever cream he's using to try and improve his complexion. And my own smells, the scent of the candles I sometimes light to freshen the room, and the pervasive odour of the quarry. I've brought it back with me: something of the dampness of the hole itself, the trickle of water through every cranny and crevice of the slate heaps; the wet moss and the slime of black mould which grows everywhere; and even a strange, cold, rusty-metallic tang I can taste on my tongue, the taste of the pool. And the rubbish. Unmistakable, the whiff of the stuff that people have thrown away. I've carried it home with me. I can smell it in my room.

I sit on the bed and eye myself in the wardrobe mirror.

David Kewish. A younger version of my dad. Well-made, with thick black hair, almost good-looking, like him. He was always Mr Kewish, even when the headmaster decided to go modern one term and said we could call the teachers by their first names. Head of English, respected by colleagues and parents. He taught at the school for more than a decade, and sometimes his students did quite well. In a good year, he'd bask in the reflection of their results and accept the congratulations of the parents. But the truth is—funny, nobody except me seemed to notice—there weren't many good years. His results were disappointing, even poor, but somehow he always got away with it, the model of a hard-working, committed teacher.

So what was the trick? How did he keep it up for years?

He had an easy smile which worked well with the parents. With his younger colleagues, he was brisk, a bit offhand, enough to keep a professional distance. With us students, he could do a convincing frown, a menacing growl or a sharp little bark when he needed to assert himself, and he was popular because he did jokes against himself, about his shabby old-fashioned clothes and the odd choice of ties he blamed on his colour-blindness. And another thing: in his thirties he'd published a novella in the *Anglo-Welsh Review*, and so he was 'a writer'. It followed that he must be an insightful teacher of literature.

He wasn't. He couldn't teach for toffee. He was kicking crap. We 'did' *Wuthering Heights* . . . He read it to us, every word, chapter after chapter, for nearly two terms. We 'did' *The Waste Land* . . . He read it to us, twice, seemed at a loss himself, and we were none the wiser afterwards. We 'did' lots of stories and poems. I mean, he read them to us. Is that teaching?

I open the wardrobe door. Dad's clothes. I reach for a hanger and take down one of the jackets he wore nearly every day at school. I close the door, slip on the jacket and look at myself in the mirror . . .

Like Dad. When people say I'm like my father, it's supposed to be a compliment, that I'm nice and polite and poised. But I know what it really means. I've got Dad's knack of looking right and somehow getting away with it.

And now I eye myself in the mirror, in the tweedy old teaching jacket which fitted Dad so perfectly. It feels comfortable on me, like a second skin. I can't help a rueful smile. No job, no place at college, but I'm a landowner, I own a slate quarry in Snowdonia. Look the part, David, I whisper to myself . . . It could've been Dad's motto.

Dad's clothes. They're all in my wardrobe. Mum had them washed and dry-cleaned after one of Kenny's scent-marking incidents, and then she brought them upstairs to my room so he wouldn't do it again. Now, the house is still and empty around me, and I need some kind of company.

Dad. Easy really. I bring him back, the look and the feel and even the smell of him.

First, I take off his jacket and put it on my bed. I undress completely—a slim angular white body, me, a teenage boy stark naked in the mirror. And then I dress myself in his clothes.

His underpants . . . extraordinary to see his yellowy stain inside them. A white cotton shirt, his tidemark on the collar and a faint blue smudge on the breast pocket where a pen must've leaked. Grey flannel trousers, and one of the brown leather belts he wore every day of his life for the past seven or eight years. Comfortable brown brogue shoes, moulded to the very shape of his feet. A green and orange tie. And the jacket again. I pick it off the bed and slip it on.

Everything fits perfectly. It all feels right . . . my fingers on the buttons as I do them up, on his shoelaces as I knot them into a neat bow, on the naff tie as I tug his familiar Windsor knot to my Adam's apple. The image in the mirror's complete.

For a long time I stand there and look at myself. Look at my dad. Smell him. These are some of the clothes he wore at school. Funny to be inside them. Not the clothes he was wearing when his car went into the quarry, of course, which are still down there, with him inside them. For a moment I imagine him wriggling and writhing and twitching in mid-air, as the car fell, and the killing impact when the car hit the water . . . imagine him struggling and sinking in icy black water . . .

The house is still and silent.

Pumpkin's asleep on the sofa downstairs. Kenny's 'working'. Simon's gone home. Mum's stitching up amputees in Mogadishu.

Dad's dead. But I feel, somehow, in his clothes, that I've got him back for a while. Silly. A silly sentimental urge that's come over me.

I slowly undress and put his clothes away again, as neatly as I can, so that no one—not even Mum—will ever know what I've been doing. I'm a bit embarrassed, even alone, and pull a funny face at myself in the mirror, so skinny and white and naked. But, as I put my own clothes back on again, I'm kind of happy with what I've done, reclaiming the territory which Kenny's tried to take away from me.

SEVEN

I decide I'll go and see Kenny 'working' this evening.

A 'ghost tour' of the medieval streets of Caernarfon in North Wales. It might be good on a wintry night, with a cold wind howling spookily through the towers of the castle and along the narrow, cobbled alleyways . . . in and out of shadowy courtyards, past the dark windows of tiny terraced houses, by the dim doorways of the pubs. But in June, when the town's as light as day at ten o'clock in the evening, when the streets are loud with teenagers and tourists and a lot of the gift shops are still open and busy, Kenny's creepy stories don't seem very creepy at all.

It's spitting with rain. I find Kenny's group, just starting the tour at the King's Gate of the castle, by the footbridge across the Seiont River. He's got a flimsy umbrella. He's wearing his denim jacket and jeans and black cowboy boots, his long hair slicked back—more like a country-and-western singer than a historic tour guide. He has about a dozen customers, and he's holding forth from the top of the steps.

'Caernarfon Castle was started in 1283 under the orders of King Edward I of England, after the death of Prince Llewelyn and the defeat of the Welsh. Llewelyn's head was carried south and stuck on a spike at the Tower of London . . .'

Kenny likes the gruesome bits. He reckons it gets the punters into the mood for his ghost tour.

'Edward II, the first English Prince of Wales, was born here in 1284. And we all know what happened to him. Yes, ladies and gentlemen, the red-hot poker . . . He was murdered in Berkeley Castle with a red-hot poker pushed into his er . . . etc. etc.'

When he spots me mingling into the back of the group, he winks theatrically. Everyone turns to stare at me, and I cringe when he tells them I'm David, his stepson. They're middle-aged Americans and Australians, a few visitors from England too, weekenders from Liverpool or Birmingham.

It's raining a bit harder, a cold spattering of rain. No sun, only a bank of grey cloud above the Menai Strait and the flat farmlands of Anglesey. There's a cormorant fishing under the bridge, sleek and black and silent, as stealthy as a submarine. There's a heron, stalking the rock pools on the other side of the estuary. And gulls, of course. The air's loud with gulls.

Kenny opens his umbrella and manages to laugh when it snaps inside out in a gust of wind. His customers grimace and turn up the collars of their jackets. He leads the group away from the castle, along the side of the town wall. He struggles to hold their attention, despite the distractions of the drinkers scurrying from the quayside and back into the shelter of the Anglesey Arms, a few braver souls huddling in corners with their fish and chips.

'Porth yr Aur, ladies and gentlemen, a place of public execution. Look up, and you'll see the gibbet, rubbed smooth by the hangman's rope. Right here, the last man to be executed in Caernarfon was hanged by the neck until dead . . . Joseph Boone, who killed a policeman in a brawl outside the Castle Hotel on New Year's Eve 1949 . . .'

To the Bell Tower, 'where a ghost still walks on winter's nights—the spirit of Samuel Pinder, washed from the decks of the trawler *Thisbe* in November 1870—and sometimes the clanging of his funeral bell can still be heard . . .'

Past our own house in Twll Yn Yr Wal, where I dread him making a ridiculous reference to the faintest of bloodstains on the cobbles, somehow embellishing the story of my finger into his mostly made-up tour . . .

Into Stryd Pedwar a Chwerch, pausing at the Black Boy, 'where the footless skeleton of a woman was recently unearthed . . . the mortal remains of Mary Cattermole, who passed away in the winter of 1832, bedridden in her cottage in the mountains of Snowdonia. Her starving dogs had devoured her feet before anyone found her. Still, on the coldest of nights, her ghost can be seen in the streets of Caernarfon, pursued by her ravenous hounds . . .'

Kenny's doing his best with the thinnest of material. His face looks cold and drawn, and his lips are cramped into a ratty little snarl, as he raises the pitch of his voice to keep his punters engaged. At every stop, on every corner where he pauses with the group and talks for a minute or two, he takes a fragment of historical fact and embroiders it into a barely believable, barely convincing ghost story.

'The gulls, ladies and gentlemen . . . the gulls are the souls of men who have drowned at sea. Look, and listen to them screaming . . .'

The tourists obligingly turn their heads upwards and into the rain, up to the lowering sky. Over the slate roofs of the Goron Fach and the archway of Porth yr Aur, the herring gulls are swooping and racing and crying so loudly that the whole town rings with their crazy voices.

'Drowned men, sailors lost at sea, haunting the alleyways of old Caernarfon ... restless souls come back to search for their loved ones, the wives and families they left behind when they were swallowed by the icy waves ...'

It's getting dark. An untimely twilight. We're in the yard of St Mary's Church, in the corner of the thirteenth-century walled town. Just then, a mob of gulls comes hurtling so fast and so low towards us that, as they pass over our heads, some of the women duck and shriek.

And another thing happens at the very same moment. As though in pursuit of the silvery, flashing herring gulls, a pair of bigger, darker gulls wheel and flap at the further end of the street. Plunging almost to the cobbles, they beat towards the group, no more than a few feet above the ground ...

The black-backs are on us.

Silent. No hysterical cries. Big, black, heavy wings, and something heavy and huge in their purpose as they come down the street towards us. They flash by in a second, in a blast of air, leaving a spatter of white and yellow droppings on the wall of the church.

The tourists gasp. The gulls are gone. Black-backs ... the biggest and meanest gulls in the world.

And then I know why they've come, the purpose of their passing. There's a plaintive, piping whistle. From behind a car parked beside the churchyard, an overfed fledgling gull appears.

My bird. It waddles a few pattering steps across the street, then it half-opens its wings and springs towards me. To me. The silly, fat baby bird crosses the street and starts to peck at my shoelaces.

Kenny calls out to me, 'Hey Dave, your young friend is welcome to join the tour . . .' and there's a feeble ripple of laughter. The bird potters at my heels as we pass through the wall and onto the quayside of Victoria Dock. 'This way, ladies and gentlemen, boys and gulls. To the morgue . . .'

The gull follows me. It's my bird, which came to me and undid the bandage from my severed finger: my bird, which is making itself at home in my guitar case. As we make our way towards the morgue, the tourists turn to me and ogle my companion. I scan the sky, in case the parent birds might come again. But the sky's empty. Even the other, commonplace gulls have fallen still.

The town is dark and cold. There's a strange silence.

EIGHT

Kenny pauses at the door of the morgue—a small, low, slate-roofed building just outside the old walls of the town, on the edge of Victoria Dock—and he turns to face his customers. He pretends to glance uneasily around him. He puts a finger to his lips as though to tell everyone to be as hushed as possible, and he takes a big old-fashioned key out of his pocket. He unlocks the door.

We all follow him inside . . . into the surrounding darkness, into the smell of a long-neglected darkness.

He fumbles for his lighter, flickering it into the shadows of the room while he tries to find the switch on the wall behind the door. Nobody speaks. At last the electric light comes on.

Not much of a light. It shows a mean, long room. No windows. A skylight in the roof, smothered with cobwebs. The smell of cold damp stone. A row of stone slabs.

'Welcome to the morgue,' Kenny begins, softly, slowly, 'built towards the end of the nineteenth century, when the town and the surrounding villages were struck by a plague of diphtheria. Many people—men and women and tragically a large number of children—were taken by the epidemic. To try and halt the spread of the infection, the morgue was built here, outside the walls of the town, and the bodies were brought inside . . . where they lay on these slabs.'

The tourists goggle and shudder. Kenny gestures at them to follow as he moves further into the room. He places his hand on one of the stones and he whispers the name as though it's a spell. 'Mary ap Gruffyd. According to the parish records from that terrible time, she was brought to rest here—on this very stone—on the night of twenty-third October 1887. She was six years old.'

He pauses for the gasp of sorrow at the awfulness of the tragedy, and he strokes the other slabs as he passes them. 'Here, Thomas Fellowes. Here, Sarah Monk. Here, on this slab, together on the afternoon of Christmas Day 1888, Megan, Myfanwy, and Margaret, the baby daughters of the Reverend Ifor Morris and his wife Susan. Scores, even hundreds, of people have lain here, and then they were taken for burial in the graveyards of the parishes in which they'd lived.'

An uncomfortable silence. The people in the group shuffle and glance at one another. Until one of them, a fat middle-aged woman with blue hair, suddenly jumps and shrieks . . .

There's a thrashing commotion at the skylight overhead. In a blur of wings and slapping feet, a huge gull's slithering on the pane of glass. And rapping, rapping so hard with a beak like iron that it seems the window might shatter.

At the same time, my gull—which everyone's forgotten while Kenny's doing his stuff with the slabs and the 'plague of diphtheria'—springs from nowhere. Galvanised into action, it starts pecking and pecking at the woman's red-painted toenails, which are peeking through her open sandals.

The woman screams. Hard and fast and accurate, the gull bangs at the toenails with its beak. She staggers away, loses her balance, and sits down so heavily on the floor that she cracks the back of her head on the nearest slab.

Still the gull bangs at her toes. Still she screams. There's blood on her hands, from her toes or from her head or from both. In another moment, her husband's driven the bird off, kicking at it with stiff, clumsy swipes of his legs. Kenny moves in with his umbrella. The bird flaps away to the door of the morgue and outside.

'Sorry, I'm sorry! Ladies and gentlemen, I'm sorry!' Kenny's shouting.

The commotion's over. The gull on the roof has gone. The husband helps his fat wife to her feet and sits her on the slab where the body of little Mary chilled and stiffened over a hundred years ago. Mewing, her shoulders heaving as she regains her breath, the woman rummages in her handbag for a handkerchief and presses it to her eyes. Then her husband takes the handkerchief and dabs at her bloody toes, as though to cool them with her own tears.

Kenny offers to comfort her too, but she wafts at him with her pudgy hands and he sidles away. He glares at me, baring his teeth and silently mouthing . . . fucking bird are you fucking stupid? The woman recovers herself enough to stand up, although she's trembling terribly, her toes are smeared with blood and there's a mess of blood in her hair. As the other punters make for the door, muttering, clearly unnerved, to get out of the morgue as quickly as they can, Kenny fixes a desperate smile on his face and tries to rally them.

'What can I say, ladies and gentlemen? The gulls are the souls of men who've drowned at sea . . . They've come to look for the loved ones they left behind so many years ago, their wives, their children, whose souls are restless in this very room . . .'

The last of his customers hurry out and into the street, glancing back at him as though he's a dangerous madman. Summoning one last effort to stop them, he calls out, 'I can explain, I can explain! The gulls have yellow beaks, with a splash of red on the lower mandible . . . when a parent comes to the nest, the chicks see the red splash and they peck at it, to make the parent disgorge the food it's brought . . .' His voice rises and quavers, pleading, pathetic. 'The bird reacted to its parent on the roof by attacking the lady's red toenails . . . I'm sorry, I'm sorry . . .'

He stands in the doorway of the morgue. The light from inside is ghastly on his face. He mouths at me again . . . fucking bird fucking bird fuck fuck fuck . . . His skin looks cold and mottled-grey, like the waterlogged flesh of a drowned man.

I'm gone. Halfway up the street, round a corner, ducking into the nearest, smallest alley. Where the gull's waiting for me. It nips at my heels like an affectionate puppy.

The rain stops. The cobblestones glisten under orange streetlamps. Together we walk through the empty streets. No sign of a footless woman by the Black Boy Hotel. No ghostly sailor clanging a bell in the Bell Tower. No grisly corpse hanging under Eastgate. And strangely, for this time of the year in this town, no sound of the gulls. An unusual silence.

When I get to our front door in Hole in the Wall Street, I look round for my persistent companion. At first I can't see it. Then, hearing a rustling in the ivy of the wall which butts our house, I see a quick, clumsy movement, and there's the gull . . . fluttering, flapping, using its feet and beak and wings like some prehistoric half-bird, half-reptile to work itself closer to the top. When it's succeeded, it stands up there, a dark shape against the night sky, and it beats its wings twice, three times, before shivering them closely around its body and settling to sleep.

I go to unlock our door. I'm mad at Kenny for being mad at me. I'm thinking of what he said to explain the bird's sudden attraction to the woman's toenails, and wondering why the bird came to our house, to our door, to me . . .

Fumbling, still unused to the tenderness of my stump, I knock it sharply against the door. The key falls to the street, ringing like a coin on the cobbles. I kneel to feel for it, where, on the evening of my eighteenth birthday, Kenny whooshed with the brush and a bucket of soapy water.

He's missed a bit. On the very bottom of the door, there's a red splash of my blood.

NINE

When I wake up the next morning, the gull's in the guitar case. Without lifting my head from the pillow, I stare at it and it stares back. It's only my foolish imagination, but the gleam of its eyes seems to challenge me. There's a connection between us. The bird's come to me . . . not by chance, but drawn to a fading reddish stain on our front door, to tap and tap at it with its bony beak.

'Go on. Out,' I say, as I swing my legs to the floor and stand up. 'What do you want anyway? Hey, my bird, get out . . .'

I have a muddle of moods in my head. There's a germ of nonsense, whispering that I'm glad to see the bird when I wake up in the morning . . . to see its eyes, its sharp grey tongue, and smell the smell of the beach. And then, the common sense that I shouldn't have a wild bird in my bedroom, a fat baby bird nestling where the guitar should be. For a moment, the nonsense is kind of delicious, and I bend to the gull to feel its breath on my fingers . . . just to be contrary, it waddles across the floor, hops onto my bed, launches itself to the top of the wardrobe and up to the open skylight. Without looking back at me, it's gone, out of the house and onto the town walls.

For the first time in weeks I pick up the guitar and sit on my bed with it. It feels perfect, a rounded armful of what I wanted so much, an armful of what the summer was going to mean to me . . . hours and days of me and the guitar, me and Simon and friends and the guitar and coffee and toast in my bedroom. But when I try to hold down a chord—to use my remaining three fingers and see if I can play any of the chords I know—the scabby stump sticks up and out like a knob, swollen and rude and just spoiling everything.

I try and try. I try to fold away the stump and start again without it. But there's nothing to fold. It's stiff. It's neither here nor there, but it's everywhere. I get madder and madder until I begin to think it'd be better if the whole finger had been squashed and cut off, instead of leaving me with this useless stupid scabby stiff stupid stump . . .

'Hey Dave . . .'

Kenny comes in. Bad timing. In a sudden, angry moment of trying anything to salvage the summer, I've spun the guitar around and I'm holding it left-handed. Kenny comes in just then.

'Great idea,' he says straightaway. He looks terrible, as pasty-grey as one of the undead he's been trying to conjure up on his tour, and his baggy underpants and Monsters of Rock T-shirt waft beer sweat and stale cigarette smoke into the room with him. He's brought me a wake-up coffee, an unexpected gesture of peace-making after the incident with the gull, but I'm not in the mood for it.

He reaches past me to put the coffee on my bedside table. 'Hey, why not try it like that, left-handed? A few days with Simon to help you, and in a week or two you'll have learned all the chords again and the two of you'll be up and running. Hey, what . . . ?'

I don't want to hear it. Left-handed? Strumming like a cack-handed spastic with my red knobby stump all rude and stupid? I stand up so fast that the end of the guitar catches the mug of coffee and splashes it everywhere, onto the guitar and the bed and all over Kenny's hand.

'Just leave it, Kenny, will you?' I blurt out. 'What the hell do you know about it? I mean, the guitar and everything! You've never touched a real guitar in your life, you haven't got a bloody clue, all you can do is your bloody aerial wanking and . . . just leave it, will you?'

He stands back, flicking coffee from his fingers. He does a mock surrender, holding up his hands as though I'm going to turn the guitar on him like a machine gun and mow him down in a hail of bullets. I yank open the wardrobe door and shove the guitar inside. As I slam the door, turn the fiddly little key and lock it, he's saying very reasonably, 'Nothing to do with me, squire. You bought yourself the guitar. But maybe you could put it in its case, and it'll keep nice and new until you get round to trying it again?'

Then he gets sarcastic and unreasonable, in a sarky, sneery, grown-up kind of way. 'Oh sorry, I forgot, of course the bird's using the case. You're going to let the guitar get all dusty in the wardrobe because your bird is sitting and shitting in the case. I forgot about the precious bird . . . Oh, and can you keep it away from me when I'm trying to do my work in the evenings, all right?'

He pushes past me and bangs the half-full mug of coffee onto the table. He spins out of the room.

I can't help myself. 'Work?' I shout down the stairs after him. 'You mean taking a few old farts round the town and telling them stupid spooky made-up stories? Is that what you call work?'

He stops and turns and looks back up the stairs towards

me, where I'm framed in the doorway of my bedroom. He's annoyingly calm, annoyingly grown up, although he looks like a ridiculous grey-haired teenager in his T-shirt and pants. 'The tours are going all right, thank you very much,' he says. 'You saw for yourself last night, until you screwed it up for me. I know you don't think much of my work, but it'll keep us going until your mother comes back. She'll be back and the three of us'll be all right . . .'

His step-fatherly calmness stumps me. It's mind-boggling . . . the idea that somehow he's manfully taking care of things while Mum's away. I suddenly miss her so much that when I mooch to the bed to throw myself onto it, my anger leaves me and I go limp. I see my silly stubborn face in the mirror, my hair all nerdy and tousled . . . a very un-grown up eighteen-year-old boy with a blotchy face and sleepy eyes. I think of the guitar locked in the wardrobe like a prisoner in solitary confinement. I look down at the guitar case, spattered white and yellow with the droppings of the bird which has spent the night in it . . .

The bird. It makes me angry. With myself. With my finger. With Kenny.

'The ghost tour was useless last night!' I yell down the stairs again. 'The bird was the only scary thing about it! Do you want me to bring it along tonight as well? And tomorrow?'

There's a long dangerous silence. I don't know whether he'll suddenly reappear and snap at me or ignore my outburst and disappear down into the kitchen. For a full minute, the silence seems to creep up and up towards me until all I can hear is my own breathing.

Then he's there again. He sneers up at me. 'Not a bad idea, David,' he says. 'That's two good ideas you've had this morning . . . trying the guitar left-handed, and using the bird on my tours. Your mummy and daddy would be proud of you.'

TEN

A plague of gulls. That's the way it's described in the local newspaper, as July passes into August and the summer holidays.

They've always been noisy, a bit of a pest, squalling and screaming around the town all day and even throughout the night ... colonising the rooftops with their nests, splattering shop windows and cars and tourists with their droppings, scrounging for food. But they're a feature of the town and have been every summer for as long as I can remember. It's more or less a tradition, that they disrupt the annual production of a Shakespeare play inside the castle on a lovely Sunday afternoon, yelling so loudly from the battlements that the audience sitting on their blankets on the grass with their sandwiches and glasses of wine can hardly hear what the actors are saying. It's almost expected, and kind of funny too, when the anniversary of the Investiture of the Prince of Wales is celebrated on 1st July and a mob of gulls hoot and cackle, as though they're laughing, throughout the whole event. And when Prince Charles himself comes to mark the special occasion and he strolls through the crowds to shake hands with the people, I can remember how loudly everyone cheers and how gamely he smiles when he's dive-bombed by the gulls, and his rather crumpled suit and the green Bentley purring along behind him are splashed with droppings ...

The gulls have been a pest for years. But a plague?

Things happen in August, and get reported in the *Caernarfon & Denbigh Herald*, which change the way the people of the town feel about their birds.

*

The first incident makes page eight. It happens on the 7th August. The gulls have been unusually loud and rowdy for the past few days. Laughing . . . yes, there's a ring of mocking laughter in the way they shout across the rooftops at each other. Rude . . . yes, it's defiant, a challenge to us humans, who scurry around on the ground beneath them, as though the gulls in their aerial kingdom are looking down and jeering. The noise is getting louder, there's no mistaking it. Even me, and everybody else who's grown up with it and lived with it for as long as they could remember . . . everyone notices and remarks on it.

A din. A racket. An earache. A growing headache.

I'm at the top of the Eagle Tower, the very highest point of Caernarfon Castle, and I see it all happen. Since I was little, seven or eight years old, I've been sneaking into the castle and up to my own private eyrie, my lookout, my secret place at the top of the world. There's my eagle, carved out of sandstone, perched on the battlements. Not really mine . . . It was put there in 1280-something by order of King Edward I to symbolise his power over the Welsh dragon. Nowadays it's so weather-beaten it hardly resembles an eagle at all, or even a gull or any kind of bird . . . just a funny old outcropping of rock, it looks fragile, as if a gust of wind or a buffeting of gull wings might knock it off. But the custodians of the castle have injected it with some kind of preservatives and it's been bound in its place with wires: a wrinkly lump of sandstone, it looks like nothing and means a lot.

A Tuesday morning, and I've used my free pass as a resident of the walled town to go into the castle, to get away from Kenny, to get a bit of air and my own space. Looking down, across the Seiont River and the Menai Strait and along the shore towards Foryd Bay, I see a young woman pushing a pram across the footbridge. She looks tiny, far below my eyrie, but I recognise her, she's Sally Morgan from Maesincla, a council estate on the edge of town. She's got her nine-month-old baby in the pram. Tagging along behind her, kicking cigarette-ends off the bridge and into the river, is her other kid—I recognise him too, the gobby redheaded moron who chucked gravel at me when I was rescuing Pumpkin from the castle ditch last autumn. I guess they've been enjoying the sunshine in Coed Elen, an old woodland of lime and beech, where the springtime garlic and bluebells have turned to grasses and ground-ivy and cool shady places. They cross the bridge, towards the foot of the Eagle Tower, more than a hundred feet below me. She pauses, near the ramp down to the Floating Restaurant, and waves to one of the waiters who's enjoying a cigarette outside the kitchen. At the same time, she hands something to the baby, a biscuit or a piece of chocolate to keep him quiet, and she leans over the bridge to chat to the waiter.

I hear the baby start screaming. And the pram's rolling away from her.

Gulls. There's a gull on the pram. No, not a gull. Gulls. No, not on the pram. They're *in* the pram, six or ten or a dozen gulls. They're in the pram and pecking at the baby's hands and face for the chocolate. The girl lunges forward to try and stop the pram, but she slips and falls.

The pram rolls down the ramp, faster and faster towards the edge of the quay and the river mouth. High tide. Deep water. The girl's screaming, struggling to her knees, slipping on the seaweedy stone. There are gulls everywhere, all around the pram and inside it . . .

The waiter's cool. He tosses his cigarette into the river, scoots around the side of the restaurant and onto the ramp, and he stops the pram. By the time Sally's stumbled towards him, he's flapped his arms at the birds and beaten them away.

I see it all from the top of my tower. For a split second, as he watches the gulls go cackling into the air and across the strait, the waiter glances up and sees me, just a moment's long-distance eye contact . . . the other kid too, his sneery white face turned up and he's pulling two fingers at me. In the *Herald* the following morning, the waiter adds a nice bit of detail to his eyewitness account: several of the birds had smears of chocolate on their white feathers, he says, and one of them had a biscuit in its beak. He adds that some of them had blood on their beaks. Indeed, the birds had cut the baby's fingers and gums.

Accompanying the article, there's a photo of the young mother holding the baby outside their house later the same day. He's waving his hands in the air, showing off the bandages on his stubby fingers. His mouth's swollen. Sally Morgan's got a terrible scowl on her face. There's something ugly and bitter in her eyes: fear.

Kenny reads the article, picking his nose at the same time. 'The gulls are a bloody nuisance, they always are,' he says. 'Worse than usual this year. People are getting seriously fed up with them.' He looks up at me. 'You've got to make sure that bird of yours stops coming into the house. And you don't want it following you round the streets either, like it's your pet or something. It doesn't look right, you know what I mean? People will think you've gone mad.'

'Yes, Kenny, I know what you mean.' I don't feel like quibbling over whether the bird's mine or not. Of course it isn't mine. I'm about to tell him it's come to me simply by chance and I obligingly removed the ring-pull from its beak. I may have saved its life but I don't expect its undying devotion forever and ever . . .

But then he says, 'This bit about the blood on their beaks? I don't think so. The guy's just trying to make the story a bit more vivid, so he looks like a hero for saving the baby. Did I tell you about the red splash on the gulls' beaks? I did? That's what he saw. Not blood.'

He says it with his infuriating tour guide's confidence, certain that he's right. Maybe he is. But it makes me think of the way in which the gull first came to me, drawn to the house by a strange kind of magnetism, to the splash of my blood on the front door.

The next incident is on page three. It's almost as if the gulls have picked up on their bit of publicity and somehow their fame is feeding on itself, gathering an odd kind of momentum. The twins Nancy and Nellie Ellison, aged eighty-eight, well-known and beloved local ladies, are sitting on a bench on the quayside near Porth yr Aur. Everyone adores them: inseparable, angelic spinsters, they were nurses at the cottage hospital for forty years until their retirement, and now they share a room in Marbryn, the old people's home on Bangor Road. Everyone knows them, I know them, Dad knew them; Mum got to know them when she was training to be a nurse. It's a cool, squally afternoon and I say a cheery hello to them as I walk along the quay towards Victoria Dock. They're resting their legs after a stroll through the town and around the castle, in a peaceful spot away from the youngsters drinking beer outside the Anglesey Arms. Nancy and Nellie say their usual things about how much I look like Mr Kewish and what a lovely man he was, and then I walk on. A hundred yards further, something makes me turn and look back to where the two old ladies are sitting.

They've both got their heads back and their eyes closed, enjoying the breeze in their hair. A breeze . . . no, there's a sudden rush of air past my own head and a big gull sweeps by me . . . black wings, white belly . . . a heavy projectile hurtling by. In a second it's onto the ladies. It swerves effortlessly. Without slowing in its headlong flight, it plucks the spectacles off Nancy's nose.

They both sit up. They cry out, feeling blindly at the empty spaces around their faces for the big whooshing thing that's come and gone in a moment. Yes, the big gull's gone. It beats into the sky, bending its wings away from the quayside and across the water. But, from behind the bench where Nancy and Nellie are sitting, a bundle of brown feathers leaps up and onto their laps and starts to peck at their panicky hands.

I start to run towards them. At the same time, I see some of the drinkers from the Anglesey Arms get up and hurry along the quay. Flailing and flapping at the young gull as though it's an enormous hornet about to sting them, the two old women stagger to the sea wall. They're wobbly on their swollen legs, giddy from dozing and then suddenly jumping to their feet, and they lean precariously over the edge to get some relief from the cold waves lapping below them . . .

I reach them first. I take Nancy firmly by the arm and turn her away from the wall. Someone else has got Nellie by the elbow. The baby gull turns its attentions from the women's mottled old hands and spongy ankles . . . It springs up at me, I feel the power of its wings buffeting my face, catch the familiar smell of its breath in my nostrils, and I strike it away. Again it springs up, and again I strike it down, so that it sprawls on the ground, tattered and raggedy, gathering itself together and finally hopping away from the growing crowd of people.

The ladies grow calm. They laugh bravely. They're game, more than a match for a pesky seagull after everything they've seen in a lifetime of nursing. They join in the cries of outrage when, as they sit on the sea wall and enjoy the attention of a dozen young men who've left their beer to come and comfort them, the black-backed gull which started everything comes flashing along the quayside and deliberately—quite nonchalantly and deliberately—drops Nancy's specs into the water just a few yards away.

It makes a funny, personal story, about a pair of popular local characters. No one's hurt. It isn't really news. One of the beer drinkers, who works as a ranger in the Snowdonia National Park, takes the opportunity to hold forth about the fledgling gull which was skulking under the bench where the ladies were relaxing. He says it's one of the chicks which are waddling around the town before they learn to fly, and the parent bird attacked Nancy because she was some kind of threat. *Larus marinus,* he says, showing off his professional expertise . . . the greater black-backed gull, the biggest gull anywhere in the world. The ranger's ten-year-old son, who's been sitting outside the pub with his parents, is ordered into the water to dive for the glasses—which he does, encouraged by the cheers of the spectators and photographed by his proud father. The boy recovers the specs.

In the following morning's paper, a shot of the beaming twins Nancy and Nellie Ellison, and the boy dripping seawater onto the quayside, accompanies a breezy article.

Which would've been nice. Except that Nellie's dead before the newspaper comes out.

ELEVEN

This is how it happened.

I go to see Nancy and Nellie that same evening. I spend the afternoon upstairs in my room, then stroll out later for a bag of chips from the fish 'n' chip shop on the High Street. It's the only shop still open in old Caernarfon. A few others, closed when the supermarkets sprang up on the outskirts of the town, were bravely reopened by arty-crafty incomers who thought they could make a living with their wishy-washy watercolours and driftwood sculptures, and then shut again when they realised they couldn't. Pubs and fish 'n' chip shops . . . They still make money and always will, but otherwise the old town's dead.

It's like this. I walk past the Black Boy and through the wall at Bank Quay. The gulls are as crazy as ever, circling and wheeling over Victoria Dock and around the morgue. A few of them try a swishing pass at my head, as though to panic me into dropping my chips onto the pavement, but I march on and on, stuffing the last bits into my mouth before scattering a few crumbs of batter behind me. A mob of juveniles brawl clumsily for the scraps, until a superb white and grey herring gull, a mature male, floats to the ground, clears a space for himself and gobbles everything. And then, before he takes off again, he opens his wings wide and throws back his head in a tremendously manic baying of laughter . . . marvellous, mad. Instinctively, I bend for a long brown feather which one of the young birds must've lost in the scuffle, and I tuck it into my shirt pocket.

I hurry away. But the feather reminds me of the funny, disturbing incident in the afternoon, and so I change direction into the supermarket on Bangor Road to buy some flowers for Nancy and Nellie Ellison.

It's seven o'clock when I go into the front hall of Marbryn Residential Home. There's a strong smell of old carpets and old furniture, lavender and boiled sprouts. The girl at reception is Bethan Llewellyn, a long-ago classmate of mine. Back then, even when we were twelve and thirteen, Bethan used to come to school in the mornings and show off her love-bites. She hasn't changed much . . . She's bigger and fatter now, with a fatter, prettier face, but she still has a rash of yellow and purple bruises on her neck.

'Oh Dave, you shouldn't have . . .' she whispers cutely, looking at the flowers. 'Are they for me?' Before I can answer, she angles her head towards the staircase and says, 'Go on up. The geriatric angels are in their room.'

The stairs are steep and narrow, with a chairlift installed. I go to the top and turn left along the corridor. I've visited the twins before, with flowers too, with fond memories of the kindness they showed my father when he was ill, so I know exactly where they live. The spongy softness of the carpet, the dinginess of the wallpaper, the stale perfume of old people and the old belongings they cling onto ... I'm familiar with it all.

Nancy and Nellie say it again, when I knock on their door and go into their room, how I'm like Mr Kewish and what a gentleman he was. I suddenly wish I hadn't come, although I hand over the flowers—an arrangement of carnations in a block of oasis—and accept the ladies' sloppy wet kisses full on the lips. Nellie puts the flowers onto the windowsill. I don't want to stay long, but they make me sit down on one of their beds and we smile at each other without really knowing what to say.

The window's ajar, but the room's stuffy, ripe with the bodily scents of the ladies and their clothes and the accumulated jumble of their long lives. My eyes trail from theirs to the knick-knacks which cover almost every shelf and ledge: shabby old things, worthless and useless things, but for the ladies, a museum of priceless memories. I'm thinking of commenting on the photographs which take pride of place—a faded black-and-white shot of the two of them, young and pretty, outside the castle on the day of the Investiture in 1969; then, middle-aged in their nurse's uniforms with a greying Prince Charles on a visit to the hospital; more recently, Nancy and Nellie in glorious colour, posing with Sir Cliff Richard outside a Methodist Guest House in Llandudno.

I'm about to say something about Cliff—how nutty-brown he is, what marvellous teeth he's got—when Nellie leans so close that I think she's going to kiss me again, says, 'What's this in your pocket?' and plucks out the gull's feather I put there.

Nancy takes it from her. She examines the feather for a few moments, turning it this way and that in her quivering, mottled old hands. She frowns at it and even sniffs it, as though it reminds her of something that happened to her recently but she can't remember what it is. She looks at me quizzically, raising her naked eyebrows, as if I might jog her memory with a clue about what the feather might mean . . . but when I say nothing, she shrugs and smiles, and she creaks around and sticks the quill of the feather into the oasis of the flowers I've brought.

'Thank you, young man,' she says. 'I'm not sure why you brought it, but it looks nice on the windowsill, with the lovely carnations.'

I stand up to go. As I do so, there's a tremendous bang. Something big and heavy smashes into the glass of the window.

A gull . . . so mad in its commotion of wings and the bulk of its body forcing itself against the window that it darkens the room. It's trying to get in. Stunned by its impact on the pane, dazed and infuriated at the same time, it batters at the glass. It thrusts its head inside, scatters the ornaments on the windowsill with a single sweep of its beak and tears at the carnations.

Nellie reels away and collapses onto the carpet. She makes no sound, either with her voice or on landing. She just folds onto the floor, strangely weightless, as though all her bones have dissolved.

Nancy springs to the window. Before I can do anything to help her, she slams it with all her strength.

The gull's head is inside. Its body and wings are outside.

For a few nightmarish, oddly surreal moments, the beak gapes and gasps, opening and closing and hissing the last of its breath. The bird seems to claw at the glass with its wings, the dying spasms of a creature broken beyond repair, and its flat webbed feet row in thin air. And then it stops moving. Inside and outside the room, it goes limp, the two parts of its being separated by the frame of the window which the old lady so sharply shut.

'Go downstairs for help,' Nancy says to me. Her voice is quiet and firm, her professional nurse's voice, not a quiver of panic. When I stare from the dead bird—which is drooling blood onto the carnations—to Nellie, who's lying so still on the floor, she says just a little bit louder, 'Young man, I'm talking to you. Go down and get help.'

I remember tumbling down the stairs. I bang my hand against the chairlift, but I'm so flustered I feel nothing. Bethan's cool. She phones for an ambulance and it's outside the home in less than five minutes.

Too late to help Nellie Ellison.

TWELVE

Her funeral's the following Saturday afternoon. I shouldn't have gone, and all the time I'm wishing I hadn't. At every point of the long-drawn-out theatrical proceedings I can feel people's eyes on me ... nervous glances, edgy sideways looks.

I don't think I'm imagining it. It happens inside St Mary's Church, in the corner of the old town walls, when a stoical Nancy is helped to her seat in the front row by a couple of elderly gentlemen. The church is packed. Every pew's full and people are squeezed into every aisle and I'm pressed against the dusty walls beneath the sunlit stained-glass windows. As she comes slowly through the door and shuffles towards the altar, she suddenly stops and swivels her head and stares at me, as though she's deliberately seeking me out in the crowded congregation. Everyone else turns too, to see what she's staring at. I remember she blinks at me. Her mouth opens and closes and reminds me of the way the gull breathed its last with its throat crushed in the window of her room. She holds my eyes, as if she's nailing a ghost, as if she's fixing my face forever into a cobwebby corner of her memory, and it occurs to me for a moment that she thinks I'm my father, because I'm wearing his jacket and shirt and tie to look smart for the funeral. I feel like shrivelling into the darkest, dimmest corner, like crumbling into dust and slipping through the cracks of the flagstones into the thirteenth-century crypt. Worse, I've got my wounded finger in a big fat bandage again—I banged it so hard onto the chairlift at the old people's home that the scab burst open—so, in the dingy shadows of the church, the bandage seems to glow, white and faintly luminous, with a blooming of blood on the tip of it. Nellie stares at it. Everyone stares at it.

After the service, I follow the procession out of town, walking with hundreds of mourners behind the cortege.

The hearse, its black bodywork almost completely hidden beneath heaps of flowers, crawls up the hill towards the Roman fort of Segontium and St Peblig's Church. From the back seat of an antiquated Daimler, Nancy peers out at the world, at all the men and women and their families walking alongside her. She waves queenly.

I find myself caught in a knot of people, stuck behind a young man and a girl pushing a pushchair. I can't get by, because cars are parked annoyingly on the pavement. As we come under the shade of the Scots pine trees, where the road crests and the ruins of the Roman fort lie to left and right, I start to squeeze past them. And the young man looks around at me, with a crooked, squinting, narrowing of his eyes, half-recognizing me like I'm an old school friend or something and trying to recall where he's seen me before. I know who he is: the waiter from the Floating Restaurant. I duck my head and hurry past him. I hear him say to the girl, 'Hey Sally, that's the weird guy I saw on the castle. He was kind of watching, you know, when the birds were attacking the baby . . .'

I walk ahead of them as fast as I can, almost catching up with the hearse, and all the time I can feel their eyes drilling into the back of my neck. I hear the girl muttering, 'He smells of bird shit . . .' as though it somehow connects me with the unsettling incident that took place that day.

Connects? Everyone knows I was with the twins when Nellie collapsed onto the floor. Nancy told the story of my visit; it was in the newspaper. A reporter took a photo of the gull grotesquely crushed in the window, its head dripping blood onto the flowers. She told him I brought the flowers—and a feather, which she says I took out of my shirt pocket and added to the arrangement of carnations I'd placed by the open window. She went back as far as the afternoon on the quayside, when, according to her, I was there when the gull whisked off her glasses and a big brown seagull emerged from underneath the bench and started pecking her hands . . .

Connects? People have seen me in town with the bird. Someone at the pub in Hole in the Wall Street has seen the bird flop out of my bedroom window, seen it hop off the town wall and into my bedroom skylight. When the reporter comes to the house to ask me a few questions, I fob him off by saying that my mum was fond of the two old ladies and so I took flowers because they were upset that afternoon. Feather? What feather? I tell him I don't know anything about a feather. He can see I'm in pain, standing at the door with a fat, bloodstained bandage on my left forefinger, so he goes away apologetically and writes his story as Nancy told it. Connected? I'm as much a part of the stories as the fucking gulls.

The cemetery's crowded too. Everyone in town, the whole population of Caernarfon, has come to pay their respects to the beloved old lady. It's a bright, breezy summer's afternoon. I find myself so close to the graveside that I can see the red clay walls of the pit, which has been neatly carved out by a mechanical digger. The headstone's black marble, simple and shiny, with only the name of the dead woman and the dates of her birth and death.

On the further side of the grave from where I'm standing, Nancy stands and peers into the hole. The coffin is lowered in. I keep my head down, not wanting to catch her eyes again. As I look at her heavy black shoes and thick-stockinged ankles, I have the sudden thought that she's standing on the very spot, next to her sister, where she'll be buried in a matter of months or maybe a few years. I glance up, from her ankles to her face. She meets my eyes and holds them for a moment, as if she's thinking the same thought. She smiles very faintly. Perhaps it makes her happy, to feel the warm, welcoming earth beneath her sensible shoes and know she has a place waiting for her, beside her Nellie.

It makes me shiver. To avoid the awful certainty in her smile, I scan around the crowd. Simon Reece, his cheeks and nose livid with spots; Bethan Llewelyn, with a rash of bruises on her neck. I nod at Brian, who winks at me. Something nudges me in the ankles, something chafes against the backs of my legs, and I turn round and glimpse the couple with the baby again ... the other kid, sneery mouth and carroty hair, is pressing too close to me in the crowd, deliberately catching my calves with the pushchair. 'Bird shit,' he whispers at me. 'Smell of bird shit.'

I ignore him. Kenny's there, looking like a crow in a black suit far too big for him, in a white shirt too big for him, the tie clumsily knotted at his bulging Adam's apple ... and I feel a jolt of anger through my body, the realisation that he's raided my wardrobe for some of Dad's clothes to wear at the funeral . . . a surge of adrenalin so sudden that I can almost jump across the grave and grab him by his horrible skinny throat . . .

But, at that moment, there's a drumming of gravel onto wood as Nancy tosses a handful of earth into the hole. She takes another handful. Her eyes are grey and very cold. They drill into mine. She raises and clenches her quivering hand, as though she might hurl the stones at me. But then she unclenches her fist, and the soil falls and rattles on her sister's coffin.

Silence. Everybody, the whole crowd of hundreds of people, seems to hold their breath. Lost in their own thoughts, all the men and women and children gathered at the cemetery murmur their goodbyes to an old friend. Nancy dusts her palms together, workmanlike, satisfied with a job well done, and then examines the redness of the clay on her skin. I look past her, up to the mountains of Snowdonia, the slabs and crags which stand sharply against the blue summer sky. She turns and looks too. Everyone looks.

The faintest of sounds, keen and restless and gradually more strident . . .

Gulls. A hundred of them? They whirl up and out of the quarry. Out of my quarry.

At first they're a grey smudge on the high horizon. And there are more. A thousand? Puthering out of the hole, they become a cloud, growing denser and blacker and more menacing.

The townspeople bend their heads and turn from the grave. They hurry away. They lower their eyes from the sky and try to muffle the cries which ring from the hillside. It's a mocking sound. Almost like laughter.

THIRTEEN

The bird keeps on coming to my room.

I shoo it out of the window and onto the town wall when I go to bed at night, and I see it hopping and flapping away from me, towards the Bell Tower and the castle itself, but then it's back again, nestling in the guitar case the following morning. I shut the window, the obvious solution, but at dawn it's rapping persistently on the pane and shadowing the glass with its wide-open wings, so I get out of bed and let it in.

I know I don't have to. But I do. I think: one night I'll squeeze out of the window and onto the wall and follow the bird, to see where it goes, to see where it roosts through the short summer nights . . . to see if it has any contact with the other gulls or even its huge, menacing parents. Parent, singular. One night I'll do that.

'Don't tell me,' Simon says. 'You've even given the bloody thing a name?'

He's dropped in one afternoon and we're up in my room. The bird isn't there, but he grimaces at the smell of it and the mess it's made in the guitar case with its yellowy-green droppings. When he asks where I've put my guitar and I nod towards the wardrobe, he turns the little key, opens the door, and takes the guitar out, without asking me if I mind. He sits on the bed and starts to retune the strings, touching them gently and expertly in just the right places and turning the machine heads.

'All right, don't get touchy,' he says. 'You keep telling me that it's not your bird, that it's not your bloody bird, that it just hops in and out of the window. But it obviously lives here, with you, in this room. Look, it's made a nest.' He leans closer to me. 'Hey Dave, I've come as a friend, to tell you something you need to know. The old lady died, she died of fright . . . You were there, with her, when a bloody seagull bloody frightened her to death, and everyone knows you've got a bloody seagull in your bedroom. They think you're mad.'

He plays an E major chord. The guitar hums, as though it's glad someone's rescued it from the darkness and it's in tune again, glad to be touched. He lifts off his left forefinger and the chord's a doomy, ominous E minor. 'And they think you smell. You smell of the bird. You smell of the rubbish tip. The quarry.'

He silences it abruptly, damping the strings with the palm of his right hand.

'So, has it got a name yet? Black-back, you reckon it's a black-back . . . so what about B.B.?' He does some bluesy stuff, bending the strings so much I think they're going to break. 'You know, like B.B. King, the legendary blues guitarist?'

I wince at him. It still irks me to see him playing my guitar, although I love the sound of it so much. The stump of my forefinger has grown a bigger, uglier scab; it's dried a rusty red and I've started to pick at the edges to see when it might want to come off. I look from the guitar—whose gleaming silvery strings Simon's bending like crazy—to the ugly stupid knob of my finger. My two birthday presents.

'I get the message,' I say. 'Kenny's been giving me earache about it too, telling me to get rid of the bird. I've told him I've tried locking it out at night and it keeps banging to get back in. He says it's bad news to have a seagull sharing the house with us and following me around in the streets when the whole town's so spooked about them. But then, at the same time, he's got this nutty idea about using the bird to sell his ghost tour.'

'What?' Simon gapes at me. 'Has Kenny gone mad as well?'

'The bird came on one of his tours with me a week or so ago,' I tell him. 'At first the customers thought it was kind of cute, especially when the other gulls dive-bombed us by the church and the bird was hopping around and squawking. Then it came into the morgue with us. It attacked an American woman. She was so upset she fell over and cracked her head on one of the slabs and everyone buggered off as fast as they could.'

Simon's still staring at me. I go on, 'Kenny was really freaked out at first. He ranted at me for ruining his tours. But now he's had this idea to get the bird involved, to get the gulls screaming around the morgue and battering at the windows and so on . . . like that story we did at school . . .'

Simon's gaping at me. He's stopped bending the strings. He silences them with his hand.

'*The Birds,*' I say. 'You know, a story we half-did with my dad at school, by Daphne du Maurier? He showed us the movie, remember? Well, Kenny suggested I bring the bird with me again, as a novelty to play up the spooky stuff in his tour, and maybe to get the other gulls going wild and . . .'

'Kenny's even weirder than I thought he was,' Simon says. 'Don't tell me, he wants you to take the bird to the morgue every night and call it Daphne.'

I grimace at him, seriously embarrassed. He crows at me, seeing from my expression that he's hit the spot. 'You're both bloody weird! The whole town's jittery about the gulls, but Kenny's doing ghost tours with a seagull called Daphne! And then every night, Daphne comes home and sleeps in your guitar case . . . and the guitar, by the way, stays locked in the wardrobe!'

There's an uncomfortable silence. This time, it's Simon who looks embarrassed.

I say to him, 'Not *by the way.* There's nothing *by the way* about it. The guitar in the wardrobe is nothing to do with the bird.' I hold up my stump. 'This is why the guitar stays in the wardrobe.'

He shrugs and stands up. He's about to open the wardrobe and put the guitar back inside, but then he changes his mind and deliberately leans it against the bed, where I'm sitting.

'I'd better be going,' he says. 'Pete Shaw's coming round this evening. He's got himself a guitar—not a nice one like yours, just a crappy thing from one of the charity shops in the high street.'

'Pete Shaw?' I'm amazed. More than that, I feel a stab of jealousy, like a real pain in my belly. 'Pete Shaw, playing the guitar? You're kidding. What do you mean? What can he do?'

Simon moves to the door and starts down the stairs. Over his shoulder, so casually that it hurts me even more, he says, 'He's pretty good. He looks a bit naff 'cos he's left-handed, but I'm teaching him a few chords and he's picking it up really fast.'

He pauses and turns and looks back up at me. 'Did you ever think about that? Starting again, left-handed? Just an idea . . .'

I hear his footsteps as he clatters downstairs to the bottom of the house and the front door. He calls up to me, 'Say hi to Kenny for me! And to Daphne!' I hear the door closing and he's gone.

FOURTEEN

Daphne or B.B. or whatever it isn't going to be called . . . I have a dilemma about whether the bird should come and go in and out of my room whenever it feels like it, or not.

Maybe Kenny's right about the bonding. It sees me

through its brand-new baby-gull's eyes as a big, friendly shadow, ever since our first meeting when I smothered it gently with the fuzzy blanket, reached into the darkness to stroke its belly for a few moments, then removed the deadly ring-pull from its beak. More than just a shadow. A living creature which saved its life.

It's been showing its attachment to me in a number of ways. It's grown jealous of the nest site it's established in the guitar case. Pumpkin's the first to discover this. She's got used to the bird being in my room when she comes for a snuggle on my bed, although she always skirts it warily and slinks up to me in an almost apologetic way. Sometimes, when the puppy comes in, the gull opens its beak wide and does the hissing yawn with its long sharp tongue, or else it snorts through its nostrils. In either case, the dog and the bird eventually settle down, the dog on the bed and the bird in its nest.

It all changes one day when the gull gives me a special present. Perhaps it's meant to show that the bird won't share me with anyone or anything anymore ... maybe, from now on, I've got to be *its* friend or companion or saviour and nobody else's.

It happens like this. I'm sitting on my bed, thinking about what Simon said, actually what Kenny mentioned a while back, about playing the guitar left-handed. Oddly, I feel even less inclined to do it since Simon's told me he has a new buddy to play with. It would look so creepy, so kind of desperate, as if I'm jealous of Simon playing with Pete Shaw and I'll do anything—even copying bloody Pete Shaw—to get back in. If I'd had the gumption to start straightaway, left-handed, as soon after the accident as I could—even while the finger was still a throbbing mystery hidden inside the bandage—I could've picked up the basic chords and made a clumsy new beginning. But I didn't. I've been moaning and moping and wasting for all these weeks, so now Simon's already playing with somebody else. And I'll look really stupid, really desperate, if I start now.

A grey afternoon. A grumble of thunder. A storm's heading in from the sea, the clouds are darkening and lowering over the town and the gulls are strangely quiet. Not silent. I hear the occasional bleating of their voices in the still air, and something irritable, ill tempered in their cries.

So I'm sitting on my bed. The guitar's in the wardrobe. I'm teasing around the edges of the scab on my stump with a pair of tweezers. Soon it'll lift right off, in one piece, like a thimble made of hard, dried blood. Underneath it, the skin'll be new and clean. It's that kind of afternoon: a time to feel grumpy and down on myself and pick at my scab.

My gull comes through the window. With one beat of its wings, it flaps from the town wall and lands in the guitar case.

'What the hell do you want?' I mutter.

It settles down, still using the long strip of bloodstained bandage as its nest material, pulling it and poking it until it's all tucked under its belly.

'I don't know why you keep coming back,' I go on. 'I never feed you or anything. You just turn up and crash out whenever you feel like it and then bugger off again. What does it mean?'

The bird stares at me. It hisses, a very offhand way of answering my questions, and then it stares back at the window. It cocks its head at the sound of thunder.

And then the big bird comes. Black-back.

There's such a bright white flash at the window that I think it's lightning. Pure white, dazzling white. A battering commotion, and the whiteness is black, then white again, and black.

The biggest gull I've ever seen is at the window. It might be trying to get in, but its wings are too huge. So it thrusts its chest into the space, ducks its head in, and fills the frame with its icy eyes and massive yellow beak. Such a beating and thrashing and bashing of a big bird in a little window, it seems as if it's forcing itself into the room . . .

Startled, I lurch backwards off the bed. I stand there, foolishly staring and making useless, feeble jabbing movements into the air with the tweezers.

It's all over in a few seconds. The black-back flings something—a squirming rubbery thing—into the room, and then it's gone. A huge unfolding of black wings, such a powerful thrust as the gull takes off that I feel the weight of the wind on my face, a dazzle of a pure white breast . . . gone.

The window frame's empty. I brandish the tweezers. And my gull, which has been cowering in the guitar case, springs out in pursuit of the squirming rubbery thing . . .

Whatever it is, it's found a hiding place under my bedside table. While the gull does all it can to push its beak and head under the table and pull the thing out, I kneel down and peer into the dusty space.

A squab. A newly hatched pigeon chick. Still alive, but only just. The big mother black-back must have snatched it from one of the smelly nests inside the castle and brought it to its own hungry chick.

I push the gull aside and peer in. The squab's naked, blind, newborn, sculling around on its poor rubbery wings.

'Get away, you greedy bugger!' I hear myself shout at the gull. I shove it away with one arm, and it reacts by banging at my hand with its beak. 'Hey, piss off!' At the same time the squab manages to row itself blindly from under the table.

Bad timing. The door opens and first of all Pumpkin comes in, followed by Kenny.

This time there's mayhem. The gull is springing around the room, blundering into the bed and my table and chair, spotting itself in the wardrobe mirror and battering at the glass with its wings. In pursuit of the squab, it nevertheless finds time to lunge at Pumpkin. For the first time, it goes for the puppy, an all-out, full-frontal attack. The little dog squeals as the big grey beak hits and hits on her nose . . . and Pumpkin, maybe experiencing a flash of the nightmare when the jackdaws ganged up on her in the castle ditch, recoils and quails in an instinctive belly-up submission. But then she recovers herself, she bristles up and goes for the gull. Good girl. She does her first real snarl since biting Kenny at Halloween, and she worries forward, going for the bird's throat.

The gull's up for it. Instead of flapping away, it stands up tall on its slappy webbed feet, opens its wings as wide as it can, hisses horribly with the scalpel-tongue sticking out, and it thrashes its wings into the dog's snarling little face.

And Kenny? And the squab?

Kenny strides into the room, blurting, 'Fucking hell, I'm not having this, I won't have this!' and other futile grown-up expressions. 'Pumpkin, out!' he shouts, trying to grab her by the scruff, and then, 'Fucking dog!' when she whirls on him with teeth bared and just misses his fingers with a loud snap. She slithers through his legs and down the stairs. 'And you! You can fucking get out too!' as he turns his attention to the bird.

Kenny's too big for it. It's faced up to the puppy, but it's no match for the looming human who's flapping at it with hands and feet and driving it across the floor, into and out of the guitar case and towards the open window.

'Out! Out! Out!' Kenny's yells in time with the flailing and waft of his arms. The gull springs for the window. It's got the squab in its beak. 'Out!'

The bird balances for a moment in the frame of the window. With a flick of its head it tosses the squab back into the room. Then, as Kenny flaps at it again and again, the gull's gone . . .

Leaving the window empty, a little square space of grey, rumbling clouds. Leaving a gift, the newborn pigeon, dead on my pillow.

FIFTEEN

It's got to go. Yes, I know. The gull's got to go.

Kenny picks up the dead pigeon and slings it out of the window and then he clatters downstairs and out of the house. No discussion, about what to do with the bird which has caused such a commotion in my bedroom and taken over as though it owns the place . . . No debate, about whether or not it has a useful purpose, I mean, as a ridiculous novelty on his tours or . . .

Ridiculous? Of course the idea's ridiculous. And for a few ridiculous, uneasy moments I find myself stewing in my bedroom. Seething. I'm really angry. No, not with the bird. I'm angry with Kenny for his boorish intervention.

It's *my* bird. It came to *my* room. Its parent brought *me* a gift. What right does he have—Kenny Phelps, my so-called stepfather, the defiler of my real father—to come barging in and throw out the bird and the gift it would've shared with me? Yes, I'll get the gull away from the house and out of town, all right? But I'll do it my own way, on my own terms, not because of Kenny Phelps or Simon Reece or any other local busybodies.

I go down to the kitchen and out into the back yard. We have a tiny space out there, where the house was built against the old town wall: a shed which must've been an outside toilet long ago, which Dad used for storing the usual Dad-stuff like half-empty tins of paint and rusting, neglected tools, and it's where I keep my bike. I wheel the bike out, through the house and the front door and into the street.

It'll be easy. I won't have to go looking for the bird. It'll find me and follow me.

'Come on, old girl,' I say to the bike, trying to calm myself, slow my breathing and my ranting. I wheel it through the town, past St Mary's Church and the morgue, onto the quayside of Victoria Dock. I hear myself, not once but several times—come on, old girl, come on—and realise that already, at the grand old age of eighteen, I'm sounding like Dad. When he taught me how to ride a bike, years ago, across the Seiont bridge and along the road beside the Menai Strait, he'd be saying things like, 'Hiyo Silver, steady on,' and making references to Champion the Wonder Horse and Muffin the Mule, some of the crusty characters from the television when he was a boy. Now I hear myself muttering the same old stuff, and I have a sudden warm and fuzzy feeling of affection for my dad. As I push the bike onto the quayside, in my mind's eye I can see his thin, worried face, his hands trembling with his first cup of tea in the morning, his fingers quivering . . . getting older and greyer, worried about me, about Mum, not worried enough about himself. I feel a fuzzy wash of love—so sudden and strong that it makes my eyes tingle—for my silly stubborn dead Dad. And because I hear myself saying his words, I realise how like him I am, and how silly and stubborn I am too.

'Stop it,' I say out loud. There's no one on the quay, no one to hear me.

I wait. I rub my eyes and the tingling stops. It's a squally evening. The thunder's rumbled away to the horizon, across the flat fields of Anglesey, where the sky's black and flickering with lightning.

I don't have to wait long. I scan the sky above my head and over the rooftops of the town. And sure enough, there it is.

So high up that it's no more than a speck in the greyness,

the adult black-back's circling and circling. No one else would've seen it. Only me. Because I know what it's doing . . . It's watching me.

Sure enough, the chick's there. With a pathetic little squeak and a beat of its heavy wings, it springs around the corner of the morgue and patters towards me. 'Hey, you,' I say, as though it's a new puppy I've got and haven't yet given a name. 'Hey you . . .' and it squeaks louder and louder and scurries the few yards between us until it's pecking at my shoe and its whole body's shivering with the excitement of catching up with me again. 'Hey, calm down,' I'm saying. 'It's only half an hour since you were crashing around in my bedroom. It's like you haven't seen me for months . . .'

Again I have a curious wash of feeling, this time for the bird. An unwanted feeling, because of what I've decided to do. Here's a baby creature, a living creature, which recognises me, which knows me and wants me. It's nibbling my shoelaces. 'Daft boy,' I say. 'Daft girl. Whichever you are. What are we going to do with you?' And I think it's me who's daft, for my funny mixed-up feelings . . . so confused about its place in my life, or at least in my summer, that I can't decide if I want the black-back squatting in my brand-new guitar case or as far out of the town as I can take it.

I steel myself. 'Come on, let's walk. A nice long walk.'

A grey evening in late summer. An eighteen-year-old boy pushing a bike. Not riding it, although the track along the old railway-line by the shores of the Menai Strait is custom made for cycling . . . a boy pushing his bike, while a fledgling seagull half-flaps and half-runs along behind him. A strange picture it would make. I keep turning to see how the bird's doing, and we walk for half a mile, another half a mile, and I keep on walking, further and further from the town. It can almost fly, I think. Still entirely mottled brown, with a grey beak and grey feet and a paler belly, it's nevertheless big, already bigger than a full-grown herring gull, an unmistakable heavyweight. Black-back. It spreads its wings and beats them with tremendous power, thrusting itself into the air for a yard or two and landing on the slappy webbed feet. So the bird follows me, leap after leap, then running, its wings closed tightly to its body, behind the back wheel of my bike.

Black-back. It'll stay dull and brown for a year, and then, in a miracle of changing from an immature bird to an adult, it'll shed its chicken feathers and be gleaming white beneath and sooty black on top. With a proud, snow-white head. With deadly, icy-pale eyes. With a mighty yellow beak. A blood-red splash on the lower jaw.

Black-back. All the time, as I walk and wheel the bike, as the young gull beats along behind me, the parent bird's there. *Larus marinus:* the biggest gull in the world. It soars above me, sometimes so high it's just a speck, sometimes dipping closer and shadowing me ... now white, now black, twisting and turning to show me its gleaming belly and sooty back.

We walk for an hour. The bird's slowing. It's tiring. Good. The cycle-track's densely overgrown on both sides with bramble and alder. We're almost four miles from home, at Felinheli, halfway between Caernarfon and the city of Bangor, a little town which used to be a busy port for the shifting of slate brought down from the mountain quarries. And it's getting darker. Because of the distant storm, still grumbling and flashing in the distance, the summer evening's gloomier than usual. There's something heavy and threatening in the gloom, although the thunder is far away. It presses on me like a lump-weight. Whatever I'm doing, whatever I've decided to do, I want to get it over with and go home.

I stop walking.

'All right,' I say to the bird. 'It was nice knowing you. But this is where we say goodbye.' I hear a little quiver in my voice, although I'm trying to sound cool. 'I don't know why you came to see me, why you came knocking at my door . . . Well, I do know, I guess,' and I hold up the stump of my left forefinger. 'Because of this? Because of the blood on the door? I don't really know. Do you?'

The gull's staring at me. Its body is heaving with the exertion of the four-mile walk, all its strenuous flapping and hopping while I've been calmly strolling. It cocks its head, angles an eye at the scab of the stump. 'Do you know why you came? Is it this? Look, you daft boy, you daft girl, take a last look . . .'

I dump the bike onto the ground and I bend to the bird, intrigued by the way its eyes are fixed on the finger.

I move the finger slowly to the left and then to the right, like an optician testing the bird's eyesight. No, like a snake charmer or a hypnotist. And the bird follows it, follows the red scab, moving its head left and right, slowly, left and right, mesmerised.

The bird's mine. Completely mine.

Not the idea. Not why I've walked all the way out of town with it, to get rid of it, to abandon it.

I hold up the finger. Stop it in mid-air. The gull freezes and stares. It doesn't seem to be breathing.

And suddenly there's such a whoosh through the air that I think a jet plane's hurtling past. The adult black-back dive-bombs at my head. I feel the pressure of its wings in all the air. It seems to suck my breath away.

Distracted, I duck for cover. At the same time I feel a jabbing pain in my finger.

Then the big gull is gone. I glance up, see it accelerating into the sky, climbing in an awesome rocket-launch until it's a speck again.

I look down. My bird is flapping away, with the scab of my stump in its beak.

I stand up quickly and look at my finger: a soft, pink

knob . . . the top of the joint, as though newborn. A closer look, angling it into the last of the sunlight, and I see a speckle of bone splinters, the remains of the crushing in the hinge of the door, tiny fragments of bone below the baby skin.

Cold. Raw. Exposed to the keen air and the salt in it.

'Hey you!' I'm shouting at the gull, bullying at it with my feet. It springs away from me, clearing the bike with a single wing beat. There, calm as can be, it flips the scab into the air as though it's just another scrap it's scavenged from a dustbin, and swallows it in one gulp.

'Hey, that's me! That's a piece of me you've just eaten! Not a bloody chip from the chip shop! Not somebody's bloody sandwich!'

Enough. If I had any doubts about leaving the bird, they're gone. I grab the bike and yank it upright. No 'come on, old girl' or 'Hiyo Silver.' I just leap onto the saddle, point the bike back the way we came, and pedal with all my strength.

'You aren't mine!' I yell over my shoulder. 'You've never been mine!' And skywards, where the parent bird is circling and calling, filling the air with hoarse, barking cries, 'He's yours! You can bloody have him!'

The baby gull makes a futile attempt to stop me. As I stand on the pedals to get as much speed as I can, it makes its biggest leap ever. It flaps and flaps alongside me, for ten or twelve or fifteen feet . . . and as it crash-lands heavily on its breast it swerves into my way. For a horrible second, there's a *clack-clack-clacking* as its beak hits the spokes and the bird's a blurry-brown raggedy thing caught in the back wheel. It falls back. I stand as high as I can on the pedals, I thrust harder and harder and hurl myself along the track.

I cycle away, with all the strength in my legs. Once, I glance back to see that the bird's on its feet and furiously beating its wings, reassured that it isn't badly hurt in the impact. But I don't stop. The wind's keen on my finger. It feels good. It feels clean and good. It gives more power to my legs and the need to get away.

To get home.

SIXTEEN

'Bits of bone. Just under the surface of the skin. Working themselves out. All part of the healing process.'

That's what the nurse tells me when Kenny takes me to the clinic to get my finger checked. She's Welsh, but quite pretty. She holds the stump under a very bright light and examines it. The swelling's gone down. It doesn't look so big and rude anymore.

'It's healing beautifully,' she says. 'Now that the scab's come off, it'll be tender for a while. It'll be ouch for a few weeks if you knock it or if you put it into water that's a bit hot or a bit cold. Maybe your dad'll let you off the dishwashing duties at home.'

I can't be bothered to tell her that Kenny isn't my father. He's sitting beside me with a silly-sentimental smile on his mouth, pretending to be proud of his bravely wounded son.

'But it'll soon toughen up,' she continues. 'Of course there'll be times when you're going to miss the top part of your finger.' And she pauses, trying to think of some examples. Unable to come up with anything, she shakes her head and goes on. 'I don't know, in a job, maybe using a computer or something . . . but the doctor's done a great job and you'll get used to it.'

Kenny winks at me. Then he changes the smile into a pursing of his lips, to show that he knows I'm thinking about the guitar and he's sharing my glumness about it. The nurse takes a pair of tweezers and angles them keenly towards the stump. Feeling me cringing as the gleaming steel hovers around the pink new skin, she says, 'I won't hurt you. You won't feel a thing. But I can get a few of these bits of bone out while you're here. That's what they want to do . . . They want to get out.'

She tweezes at the splinters. She doesn't hurt me, although Kenny squeezes my elbow as if I'm a soldier having a bullet dug out of my arm. As one of the tiny white pellets flips out of the stump and off the table and disappears into the deep carpet, she giggles and says, 'Oops, never mind . . . It'll get hoovered up in the morning, unless it's nibbled away by the dust mites before then. How did the scab come off, by the way?'

'I suppose he was picking at it, you know, like boys pick at things,' Kenny says.

I haven't told him how it happened. Inside my head, I say to the nurse, 'It was pecked off and swallowed by a greater black-backed gull, and now you're feeding bits of my bone to the dust mites in the carpet . . . Good to know that the local wildlife's getting the benefit of my injury.' But I don't really say anything.

A few days have gone by since I took the bird out of town and came racing back on my bike. Kenny hasn't mentioned anything about it, although he's popped in and out of my room as usual with an odd cup of coffee and to try and have a chat. Everything in the room's exactly as it was when the bird brought me the squab as a present. Like most teenage boys, I don't do a lot of tidying. There are magazines and bits of my clothes scattered around, and the guitar case is open on the floor—the splattered droppings, which the gull's pressed into the velvet lining with its feet and belly, have dried into a kind of crumbly brown cake. The air's fresher, though. It's late August, towards the end of a long hot summer, and I keep both of my windows open day and night, the bigger one overlooking Hole in the Wall Street and the pub opposite, and the skylight, so a sweet breeze swirls through the room all the time.

Neither of us mentions the bird. As far as Kenny's concerned, he manfully bundled it out of the window and it hasn't come back. So that's all right. I'm thinking it's followed its parent along the track to Felinheli—the nearest town with chips and pizza crusts scattered around the dustbins—and that's all right too.

'Show me,' he says, and without waiting for me either to agree or to try and stop him, he stands up from my bed and crosses to the wardrobe. 'The guitar . . . I mean I know I'm a piss-artist and I can't play a note myself, but I want to see what you can do and what you can't do. You can't just leave it in here forever, hidden away as though you never got it. So, now that your finger's healing up, let's check it out.'

He's been trying, in his weasly roundabout kind of way, to 'have a talk about things'. About our summer. About his castle tours and ghost tours. About my accident. About Mum. He tells me he's tried to call her to find out if she might be coming home. And I've been staring at him, goggle-eyed and open-mouthed, waiting for him to tell me what she said . . .

But he doesn't. When I give up waiting and blurt out, 'So? So did you speak to her?' he just shrugs and mutters vaguely about the impossibility of contacting her and maybe she's been kidnapped by Somali pirates and sold into a harem or something . . . until he runs out of steam and changes the subject completely.

'Show me.' He jumps off my bed and turns the fiddly little key in the wardrobe door. 'The guitar, I want to see what you can do and what you can't do.'

He can't resist eyeing himself in the mirror, turning his head one way and another to get a look at both sides and stroking the grey stubble on his chin. Then he takes the guitar out of the wardrobe, hands it to me, and sits beside me on the bed. Too apathetic to resist, I decide to humour him for a while.

The guitar's gone out of tune since the last time Simon came, but as soon as I retune it I find I can't do any of the chords I've learned. Hopeless. I can do E minor. For all the others, the damaged finger just gets in the way. Nothing to do with the tip of it being tender if I try to hold down a string on the fret-board ... it's a straight, stiff piece of my hand which won't bend anywhere near the fret-board in the first place.

'Sounds cool,' Kenny says, completely and utterly in-appropriately. 'What's that chord you're playing?'

'It's E minor,' I reply. 'I can play it beautifully, probably just as well as Jimi Hendrix ... I mean when he was alive, before he choked to death on his own vomit. But it's the *only* chord I can play. Not many songs use E minor all the way through. Maybe I should write one?'

He doesn't get the sarcasm. He nods enthusiastically. 'Strum it, Dave, use the plectrum, give it a bit more oomph ...'

The plectrum's stuck in between the strings above the nut, near the machine heads. A little triangular piece of red plastic. I take it out and start to strum.

Sad. E minor is a doomy chord anyway. Even sadder and doomier when it's strummed over and over again, with the celebrated air guitarist Kenny Phelps sitting next to you and nodding his head with his eyes closed and drumming his hands on his knees like a hippie at an open-air rock concert.

He suddenly stops and stands up. I stop too. The dirge is awful. He rubs his hands together and grins at himself in the wardrobe mirror. 'Well anyway, it's a start. Don't you think so? Better than nothing? Better than just locking it away? The guitar's out of the closet, as they say, literally and metaphorically.'

Pleased with himself for helping me to confront the situation, and no doubt congratulating himself on being a caring and proactive stepfather, he turns out of my room and goes downstairs.

Just to be contrary, I turn the guitar round on my lap and hold it in the left-handed position. As an experiment, I try to form a chord on the fret-board, using the fingers of my right hand. They're unfamiliar, really clumsy and diffi-cult, refusing to go where I want them to go. I try E major and then C, and my fingers struggle against me, bending into position then springing out. It's like starting again. I huff and puff for a minute or two, until I glance up and see my silly boy's face reddening in the mirror, and suddenly I can't be arsed.

Unfair. When I hold the guitar close, and I inhale the new smell of it, the smell of the thrill of my eighteenth birthday and the loveliness of the present I bought myself, I feel a tingle of tears in my eyes. But I don't cry. I don't want to cry. I'm angry and fed up, the bagpipe drone of E sodding minor is still ringing in my head. And left-handed? Starting all over again, left sodding handed? I can't be arsed.

I open my bedside drawer, drop the plectrum into it. Slam it shut.

I open the wardrobe, shove the guitar into it. Slam it shut.

SEVENTEEN

To get away, to get away from Kenny and the guitar and the house and its emptiness, to get away from the wardrobe in my room with my dad's clothes in it ... I go up to the quarry to breathe some air in the mountains and talk to Brian.

It's evening when I jump off the bus and walk up the slatey track. Late summer, and all the foliage of ash and oak and rowan is a darker, dustier green. The freshness of spring is long gone. August, and already in the weight and density of the leaves there's a strange torpor. Not even the drowsiness of summer, but somehow a sickliness. A landscape of living things, nodding into the sleep of autumn. The wintry sleep of death.

And already, two months since the longest day, the light's fading at eight o'clock. Not a gentle summery dusk, but a chill grey light from the dead weight of the slate, from the spoil and the slabs long ago discarded from the disused quarry.

No birdsong. Not a breath of air.

As I walk through the tumble of boulders and the shade of the mountain ash, the only sound is the sudden clatter of a magpie out of the bracken. A stink from the place where it's been. Curious, I push into the undergrowth. A great roaring cloud of black flies erupts ... from a dead sheep, a swollen carcase of matted brown wool, oozing gas. The magpie's had its eyes.

Brian's neat little car is in its usual place. The caravan door's open. The radio's on, the smooth brown voice of an actor reading a story. I walk to the edge of the quarry and look down. Yr Twll. The water level has dropped, after weeks of a hot dry summer, and the bonnet of Dad's car juts above the surface. The paintwork is matt and mottled. The chrome of the radiator grille is orange, where the underwater slime has dried in the open air. Still the windscreen's submerged, only just. For a moment my stomach lurches ... As the light plays on the surface, as a shadow of cloud moves across the water, I imagine the figure of my father, broken, slumped at the wheel.

Unnerved, I cross to the caravan and look inside, thinking to surprise Brian with his eyes closed, his head on the pillow of the narrow bed, lost in the radio's hypnotic drone. But he isn't there.

The newspaper is spread on the table, the dictionary open beside it. His reading glasses. A cup of tea, still warm. The kettle, still hot on the gas ring. A vase of wild privet, its giddy, overwhelming scent. His binoculars . . . no, they're missing from the hook by the door, where he usually hangs them on their leather strap.

I sit on his bed and turn off the radio. Something about the quarry has unsettled me: maybe the quietness, the deadly dryness, the metallic smell of the water in the deep hole and the rancid rubbish which has been tipped into it. As I look around the inside of the little caravan, all of Brian's nice things and even the fragrance of the privet seem to fade and disappear and I see it as I'd first seen it . . .

When Dad drove me up to the quarry for the first time.

A normal school day, a year ago. Four o'clock on a summer's afternoon, and as usual I wait for him while he goes back to the staffroom with his books and papers and sorts himself out before he's ready for us to go home. All my friends and the other students have gone, and I've been reading a bit in the empty classroom before I saunter to the car and wait for Dad to come. At last he's there. We jump in and drive out of the school, through Bangor and its outskirts and on the road towards our home in Caernarfon.

But then he turns away from the coast, away from the coast road we always use after school on a normal afternoon, and we're climbing into the foothills, through the village of Caeathro and then Waunfawr, where Snowdon and Mynedd Mawr loom against a grey sky.

Where are we going? He says he wants to show me something, he wants to tell me something . . . that's all he'll say about our detour, and we climb more steeply into the mountains.

So this is the first time I've been to the quarry. Dad

bounces the car up the track and stops with a sudden, ratchety jerk of the handbrake. And what's this? I ask him, but he's already out of the car and striding away to the edge of the hole.

I stand there with him, beside him. I remember I can smell him, the scent of his body after a long day in school, and I can smell the water a hundred feet below us. It's a drizzly, mizzling summer, and the walls of slate which rise high above us and encircle us seem to blur into the lowering clouds. I remember I can smell his body more keenly than I remember before, and his weird tie—a kind of puce with splatters of red like blood or gravy on it—seems even odder than it usually does, in the unfamiliar, dank and dreary place.

He turns to the caravan, unlocks it with a little key and we go inside. It smells horribly of damp and decay, as though generations of small animals—mice or snails or armies of ants—have snuffled and slithered and nibbled and gnawed and eventually died there.

Dad sits me down, takes a deep breath, and tells me.

Firstly, he tells me that the quarry's been in the family for a hundred years, he owns it, he's never done anything with it or had any use for it, but from now on it's mine. Secondly, he tells me he's ill, he's really ill, as bad it can possibly be.

How to react? What do you say when your father drives you up to a slimy hole in the side of a mountain, a sinkhole of slabby cliffs and green-black water, and tells you he's dying?

I'm embarrassed. A strange sensation. I should be shocked, or stricken by an overwhelming feeling of the grief my mum and I'll experience when he dies in a few weeks' or a few months' time. But no, I squirm on the edge of the bed, I squirm with embarrassment, and he does too. I remember how clumsily I try to change the subject, as if my father telling me he's dying of colon cancer is kind of annoying and I've got more interesting things I want to talk about. I blurt out, 'Hey Dad, that tie, how many times has Mum told you not to wear it?' And he brings it back to his preferred topic of conversation, with a painful joke about his colour-blindness ... that he's going to die of colour-blindness after all, ha ha, the blurring of red and brown he's experienced all his life and so he never noticed the spotting of blood in his stools until it was too late and now the cancer's untreatable.

Then he stands up sharply and ducks out of the caravan, leaving me sitting on the damp little bed.

I watch him stride to the edge of the quarry hole, to the same spot we'd been standing a few moments before. He looks so thin and frail. His schoolteacher jacket and grey trousers are baggy on him. His shirt collar's too big on his shrunken neck. He's a dying man, contemplating the prospect of his own death. I wonder if he's broken the news to Mum and what she said, and how they decided to break the news to me. He shuffles another pace forward, and for an awful moment I think he might hurl himself to a quicker death, down and down to the jagged slate boulders in the pool. But then he shuffles back again, away from the brink. He moves out of my vision, out of the coffin-shape of the caravan door in which he was framed.

I just sit there. I don't know what to say or think. The sense of embarrassment leaves me and I wonder mundanely what we'll talk about on the drive home and what we'll do when we get there. Homework, dinner, washing the dishes? A bit of telly and off to bed? A normal evening, after this? After telling me this?

I hear Dad open the car door. I hear the door shut and the engine start. He peeps the horn, so I get up and out of the caravan.

What happens then? I close the caravan and try to turn

the little key. Fiddly thing. Before I manage to lock the door properly, I see in the corner of my eye that the car's already moving forward and Dad's going to turn round so we'll be ready to go out of the quarry.

I slip the key into my pocket—after all, it's my caravan in my quarry—and make for the car.

And then Dad waves at me. I see the strange twisted expression on his face. He's laughing or crying or trying to laugh through a blur of tears, a look of pain and confusion and anger and disappointment all blurred together. He pips the horn again. A silly cheery sound, it echoes sharply from the walls of the quarry.

The engine roars. Maybe the sole of his shoe is wet and his foot slips off the brake and onto the accelerator? The car lurches forward. The tyres squeal and it speeds towards the quarry. A second later, engine screaming as if the throttle's jammed to the floor, the car leaps over the edge.

It falls. No twisting or rolling in mid-air. The weight of the engine keeps it straight and true. The car falls and falls, bounces off the side of the quarry and smashes into the pool.

There's a tremendous impact, a shock of sound. A crack of metal on grey, unforgiving water and a churning of silvery foam. All in one mad and mysterious moment. And then a sudden silence.

If there's an echo I don't hear it. As though the hole is accustomed to having strange and unexpected things thrown into it, it swallows the car with a terrible nonchalance. Less than a couple of seconds after Dad's waved and grimaced at me and cheerily piped his horn, he and his car are gone. The quarry is utterly quiet. The water is so completely still that the clouds are reflected in it.

I stare into the hole. For another unreal moment, separated from reality by the suddenness of what's happened, I think of throwing myself into it. I remember running blindly around the edge of the quarry, shouting 'Dad Dad Dad' with some vague notion of finding a way of slithering down, of getting down to the pool and plunging in and diving to the car and . . . But the edges are sheer, it's impossible. The water a hundred feet below me is a different world from my world of bracken and woodland and I can never go there unless I take the dive that my father's taken . . .

I remember running to the caravan, fumbling to unlock it and letting myself in, not knowing why I'm doing it or what I'll do once I can throw myself inside. Rolling onto the bed, I curl myself into as tight a ball as I can and squeeze my eyes shut, to try and blank out the image of what I've just seen . . . I press my hands to my ears to deaden the crack and smash of the impact . . .

Brian comes in. No, not then, not the afternoon my dad went into the hole. But now. He comes in and finds me lying on his bed, curled into a ball and replaying inside my head those dreadful moments.

'You all right?' he asks. I sit up sharply, blinking as the inside of the caravan and all of Brian's neat and homely things come back into focus. He snags the strap of his binoculars onto their usual hook. 'I was up on top of the quarry. I thought I heard the peregrine and went up to see if I could see him. No luck. But I was watching you come up the track, saw you stop and take a look at that stinky sheep.' He eyes me queerly. I'm rubbing my eyes with the heels of my hands. 'What's up? You been crying? Been getting more earache from Kenny?'

'I got a headache,' I said. 'No, not Kenny. Your flowers. I kind of like the scent but it gives me a headache . . .'

He sits next to me on the bed. Concerned for me, he puts his hand under my chin and angles my face towards his, as though I'm a child. He looks very deeply into my eyes, searching for the truth, and says, 'I'm not sure I believe you. Do you want me to drop by your house sometime and have a chat with Kenny? Or maybe I could tag along on one of his tours one evening and then have a friendly word with him afterwards?'

He makes a fresh pot of tea. It's a lovely evening. We carry our cups outside, to get some air and clear my head, and we stroll to the edge of the quarry. Brian's burbling something about the drop in the water level and how the poor old car looks as though it's trying to crawl out of the hole . . . until I nudge him to be quiet and turn my head up towards the sky.

The peregrine is wheeling high in the murky clouds, and a pair of ravens is mobbing it, in a lazy, friendly kind of way. The falcon flicks this way and that, with the easy rhythm of a skater on mottled grey ice. The ravens tumble and flip, a couple of clowns. Brian and I stare up and say nothing, only he gasps when the peregrine evades its amiable tormentors with an effortless dive, plunging so swiftly that it's gone in a moment, out of the sky and lost beyond the horizon of the quarry.

'Marvellous,' Brian says. He scans around him, from the clouds and around the cliffs and down to the water far below, as though he's the owner of the quarry, not me. 'Hey, I just realised why it's so quiet today. No gulls.'

He puts his arm around my shoulders and walks me back towards the caravan. 'I'm so used to the gulls being here a lot of the time, that when they aren't I wonder what kind of mischief they're up to. It's too quiet. I mean, after the nasty business with the Morgan baby, and then dear old Nellie Ellison . . . I wonder who's going to be next?'

EIGHTEEN

'No, not earache. I'm well and truly, one hundred per cent, literally pissed-off with him.'

I bump into Brian in town a few days later and start to tell him about Kenny. The first thing he does, as though we're in the caravan and he's going to reach for his big old dictionary, he frowns and wags a schoolteacherly finger at me and he says, 'No, David my boy, you can't be *literally* pissed-off with somebody. It couldn't possibly make any sense at all. Metaphorically maybe, but not literally.'

So I put him right. We're in Castle Square. He's walked into the town centre from his flat on Victoria Dock, to pick up his pension from the post office. He can see straightaway that, despite the summer sunshine and the holiday atmosphere in the busy streets, I'm smouldering mad.

He buys me a burger from a market stall—he's feeling rich, he says—and he sits me down on a bench. My hands are trembling. A squelch of tomato sauce drops onto the front of my shirt when I take my first bite.

'Tell me everything,' he says. 'Messy boy.'

So I tell him. Last night, I'm asleep upstairs in my bedroom. Midnight, I hear Kenny come stumbling into the house and up to his room, so I know he's been at the pub for a Friday lock-in with his mates. I wait until the house is quiet again and I go back to sleep. When I wake again very suddenly and see the moon framed in the skylight right above my head, I know that somebody or something's moving around in my room.

I hold my breath and listen. 'Pumpkin?' I whisper. I think maybe she's slipped upstairs from her usual place on the living room sofa, to join me for a bit of company. I hear a movement across the room, as though she's flopped down on the floor by the open window. 'Pumpkin? You OK?'

Or maybe it's the gull. The skylight's open and the bird could've hopped from the town wall onto the roof and into the house. So it's back. What's it doing? Trying to open the wardrobe with its pesky inquisitive beak? The moonlight, reflected in the mirror, swings across the wall as the wardrobe door creaks open.

I sit up in bed and blink and rub my eyes. It's Kenny.

I can hardly believe what I'm seeing. Dressed only in a black T-shirt, his legs all white and skinny and hairy, he's opened the wardrobe and he's staring into it.

'Kenny?' I hiss at him. 'What are you doing, Kenny?'

He ignores me. He stretches both arms lazily above his head so that the T-shirt rides up and reveals his skinny white hairy bottom, and he starts to piss into the wardrobe.

A yellow arc of piss. Golden in the moonlight. A steamy rainbow.

I leap out of bed and lunge towards him. He's pissing long and hard . . . not aiming, not using his hands at all, just stretching and smoothing back his hair with both hands and jetting the hot powerful piss all over Dad's clothes and into the open round mouth of my guitar.

A pungent whiff of beer and ammonia. The jet drumming loudly. The strings humming.

'Fuck you, Kenny!' I grab him and wrench him away from the wardrobe. He doesn't seem to feel me touching him. The jet keeps on coming, more powerful than ever, as though it'll never slow down and stop. 'Bloody hell Kenny!' I'm shouting at him, 'Bloody hell!' into his face, into his ears, but he just smiles blissfully, as though the sensation of relief is pure and lovely and nothing can distract him from it. I slap him, I tweak his nose, wasting time when I should be trying to deflect the stream of piss away

from the wardrobe, anywhere, maybe out of the window
or . . .

He's fast asleep. I shove him towards my open window
and try to aim the jet through it. Can't. It just spatters onto
the sill and all over the bedroom floor. For a millisecond I
reach for his dick, grab it all gristly and hot and squirmy,
and point it outside, and then let go and recoil. Flailing
around for inspiration, what to do, I gawp across the room
for something to help me.

Inspiration. Jimi Hendrix. The rolled-up photo on my
bedside table.

Steeling myself, as the piss splashes and scalds on my
hands, I fit it onto Kenny. I force him a step closer to the
window and point the jet outside.

His saintly smile turns into a big, open-mouthed grin.
Still, his eyes are strangely blank, unseeing, not awake to
the real world. He stretches again, luxurious as a leopard,
and pisses and pisses onto the cobbles of the street below.

At last the flow slows down and stops. I wait a few cau-
tious moments then shake the hot plastic tube until the last
amber drops fall out.

That's it. What to do? I turn Kenny away from the
window and lead him downstairs, as gently as if he's an
incontinent geriatric, and into his own beer-stinking room.
Backed up against his bed, his knees give way. He topples
flat out and lies there twitching like a man executed by
firing squad.

For a minute I just stand and stare at him. The house is
dark and silent. Outside, the world is silent and dark. I stare
at Kenny Phelps, an uncomfortable mixture of feelings
jumbled inside my head: anger, hatred, disgust . . . twinges
of pity.

And then? It takes me an hour to make my bedroom
habitable again. I bundle all of my father's clothes into a
pillowcase. Using all kinds of detergents and bleach, I swab

and wipe and spray in and around the wardrobe and the window, holding the guitar outside and tipping it this way and that to drain it, then trying my best to wipe it out and spray it . . . until at last I've done as much as I can and I collapse into my own bed again.

The moon's passed over. The skylight's a blue-black hole in the ceiling above me.

Brian's staring at me, aghast, as I tell him all this. When I pause, he says very softly, 'And today? Have you seen him this morning?'

This morning? I tiptoe past Kenny's room, hoping he's still asleep so I can get out of the house without talking to him. I glance in as I go by. He's lying flat on his back, just as I left him . . . but stirring awake with a hangover and a hard-on and the Jimi Hendrix photo still stuck on his dick. Hearing my footsteps, he jolts up and sees me looking in. The photo is erect and bobbing, he tries to yank it off but can't because he's swollen inside it . . . and he snarls at me, 'Ha ha very funny, just stay out of my room, all right?'

Brian and I sit side by side on a bench in the sunshine of Castle Square. My hands have been trembling more and more, with anger and shame at the same time, so that more squelches of tomato sauce have slopped onto my shirt. Brian's got angrier and angrier too, until at the end he's jumping to his feet and spluttering, 'He told *you* to stay out of *his* room?' To calm him down and make him laugh, I do my new party trick. I stick my stump into the remains of the burger and pull it out again—a mess of gore as though my finger's just been ripped off—and prod it at his face. He grimaces and sits down, still spluttering and speechless.

Saturday morning, market day in Caernarfon.

Nothing spectacular, not Paris or Rome or even Llandudno, but a small-town buzz of necessary business . . . the voices of hawkers and a twang of country music, a puthering smoke from barbecues, the sizzle of satay and slivers of kebab ... local people doing local necessary things as well as tourists who've come thousands of miles for the castle and the quaint cobbled streets of the medieval walled town.

The sun's hot in a clear blue sky. Not a sound or a glimmer of the gulls ... Perhaps they're out at sea, scavenging the sandflats of the Strait or the dunes of Newborough Warren ... but the swifts, the marvellous miraculous swifts, are screaming through the stalls of fruit and vegetables, swerving over clothes and shoes and CDs and videos, zigzagging by bunches of flowers and potted plants, hurtling like hooligans and spattering their droppings on sides of beef and moist, pink pork ...

We walk among the stalls. Brian pauses in the shadow of the statue of Sir Huw Owen—'teacher and philanthropist'—and, as though inspired by the inscription, buys an armful of lupins and thrusts them at me ... 'to sweeten your room, take them, please take them, you poor boy ... to sweeten your day, your summer, your life.' He's outraged by what I've told him. His eyes glisten with tears. His voice trembles a bit.

There's another voice, a wheedling voice which cuts through the noises of the market.

Brian spins away from me and hurries towards it. I follow him, trying to keep up as he pushes past a queue of women waiting patiently at the butcher's, as he nearly overturns a child in a pushchair as he forces his way by. And when we burst out of the crowd on the other side of the market and find ourselves under another statue—David Lloyd George shaking a futile fist into thin air—there's Kenny high up in the Queen's Gate of the castle, in full flow with a group of tourists.

He's standing on the edge of the balcony, and his punters press around him. Hard to make out exactly what he's saying, although his voice is so nasal that it jars on the other noises of traffic and people and the cries of the swifts. But I know the castle tour, and I know he's encouraging the tourists to stand at the front of the balcony and regally wave, just as Prince Charles waved on that very spot on the day of his investiture as Prince of Wales on 1st July 1969. Yes, they're waving, and Kenny's grinning his yellowy fangs and running his fingers through his lank, grey hair, a drooping middle-aged air guitarist in denims and cowboy boots ... an unlikely authority on the history of such a grand and significant event.

Brian's yelling up at him, angrier than I've ever imagined he could be.

Softly spoken, gay Brian ... Radio 4 and Telegraph crossword Brian, lover of birdsong and wildflowers and all the clouds in the summer sky ... he's bellowing furiously at Kenny and waving his fists just as futilely as David Lloyd who's towering over him. I stand there hugging my lupins. He leans to my ear and he hisses, his eyes still teary with anger, 'I'm not bloody surprised you want to bloody kill him! Don't worry, I won't tell anyone you told me ...'

No one around us can hear what he's saying. Indeed, at that moment, probably none of the customers on Kenny's tour can hear what he's telling them—because there's a sudden rumbling commotion in the market place and everyone turns to stare.

A fire engine is nosing into the square, past Paternoster buildings and Castle Pharmacy and the memorial to all those who fell in the First and Second World Wars. It nudges past the crowded stalls and almost to the very spot where we're standing.

Brian groans at me. 'Oh my Lord, this'll be fun ... a publicity stunt for market day ... supposed to impress the locals and give the tourists something to write home about ...'

The fire engine pulls up by the Lloyd George statue. The crowds in the market, the people high in the Queen's Gate and all along the battlements of the castle, everyone stops what they're doing to see what the fire crew's going to do. Three firemen, bulky like robots in their big black coats, get out. A voice crackles through a loudspeaker, the voice of the fire chief hidden in the cab of his mighty machine, asking the crowds to stand back and keep their distance; and with a great whirring and clanking of invisible motors, the engine erects its ladder.

Up and up it goes, and everyone cranes their necks to see. At the top of the ladder there's a fireman, heroic against the clear sky, clad in a heavy waterproof and wearing a big yellow helmet ... holding a hose which dangles down and is attached to a hydrant on the pavement. When he's higher than the highest rooftop, right up against the chimneys of the Castle Hotel and the fine tall terrace of houses overlooking the castle and the harbour, there's a breathless pause—just long enough for Brian to murmur, 'Here we go, this'll be a right bloody mess'—before the hose wriggles and writhes and spits a jet of water.

The fireman aims his hose at the chimneys and rooftops. Not a spray. A blast as powerful as water cannon.

'What are they doing? Is there a fire?' the tourists are asking, thrilled and bewildered by the unexpected action. 'No, not a fire ...' Brian's swivelling his busybody head to inform the wide-eyed visitors, 'the gulls, the gulls, they're clearing away the nests of the gulls ...'

In a matter of seconds, the roof of the hotel, the roofs and gutters of the solicitors and dentists and doctors who occupy the most prestigious addresses in town, are cascading water onto the pavements and cobbles of the square. The crowd's agog. There's a great muttering and mooing which grows into catcalling and yelling, cries of abuse or encouragement.

A marvellous disharmony in the voices . . . disgruntled locals shouting, 'What a stupid time to be doing it! on market day, on a Saturday!' . . . the cynics sniping about 'a big song-and-dance to impress the taxpayer' . . . happy-go-lucky Aussies pointing their cameras and laughing, 'Hey this is fun!' . . . Americans moaning, 'You crazy Brits, you get the first decent day of summer and you call out the fire engine to make it as rainy and grey and shitty as possible!'

Grey and shitty, the stuff that comes off the roofs.

A horrible slurry from neglected gutters. It's a splattering of toxic rain, the claggy run-off of long-ago winters, the debris of long-ago summers . . . the gulls' nests which the fireman is targeting, lumps of grasses and seaweed clotted with bird shit and regurgitated, half-digested matter . . . dead birds and fish, pieces of dead birds and fish, feathers and fur, gluey bits of bone and gristle which've been on the rooftops for months and years and baked in the sunshine, stewed in persistent Welsh drizzle, re-eaten and sicked-up a hundred times . . .

Now it all splashes from the slates and falls to the streets below.

No gulls? The gulls come back. Summoned by a common sense of emergency, they've returned from the dunes, the estuary, the quarries and lakes in the mountains. Where the sky was blue, blurred by the jet of water, suddenly there's a whirl of black and white and grey wings. A hundred gulls come brawling into town.

Man against gulls. It's a battle for territory . . . the territory of gleaming slates and overflowing gutters, the rooftops and chimney pots of Caernarfon.

The crowd surges around us. I feel Brian's arm loop through mine, as though he might save me from the crush. He's yelling, 'A mess, a bloody mess! I told you, I told you!' The lupins are flattened against my chest as more people shove closer, to avoid the spatter of horrid black

water from the buildings and the flow of it off the pavements and pooling underfoot, or to go forward where the
action's thickest, close to the rumbling motor of the fire
engine, to peer upwards where the fireman and the gulls
are joined in combat. We all look up. On top of his ladder,
the man's ducking and dodging and flapping a free hand as
the gulls beat at his head. His helmet dislodged, momen-
tarily blinded, he grabs for a hold on his gantry and the
hose sprays wildly around him, writhing away from him
and then around him like an enormous snake. He recovers
himself, the crowd gasps, he grapples the hose under control and jets the gulls and drives them back, three of them
broken by the blast and spiralling down, crash-landing on
the pavement.

The air's a whirl of wings and water, a filthy rainbow. I
blink upwards into it, shielding my eyes with one hand.

Brian shouts, 'Hey, watch out!'

And something big and black falls from the roof. Tumbling, spinning, heavy and hard, it cuts this way and that
through a flurry of feathers. A dead weight, like a blade.

Brian pushes me out of the way. The slate strikes him
and he slumps to the ground.

The crowd surges back and away from him. A space
opens around him and grows and grows, because the
blood pools so quickly and darkly and thickly that people
recoil from it. I'm the only one who stays by his side. Dropping the lupins, I kneel to him, my hands in the sticky hot
blood, and turn up his face to see what's left of it.

Hard to tell exactly where the blood's coming from.
The slate, quarried over a hundred years ago and shaped
into a thin cold slice, has shaved off his left ear ... more
than that, it's split open the left side of his head, as keenly
as if he's been struck by a guillotine. And then, an unstop-
pable weight, it's carved into his shoulder, through to the
collarbone, before hurtling onwards and smashing on the

ground. Blood—a lot of blood—is pulsing from the mash of his head and the split-open notch in his body.

Sharp grey splinters, shattered into a million pieces on the cobbles.

He's alive. Horribly injured, gaping, gasping, gagging on a bubble of blood. The firemen pull me aside. Keen to show off their public-spiritedness, now they've got a real chance to test their skills and their expensive equipment. Doubling as paramedics, they struggle to staunch the wounds. And then, when an ambulance arrives and takes Brian away, they retract their ladder and turn the hose onto the strange brew they've puddled onto the slabs and cobbles of Caernarfon Square ... mangled seagulls, broken and dead or squirming in the throes of death ... a slurry of mucous grey matter from the roofs ... blood ... so that everything, feathers which were white, water which was clean, is foaming red and gurgling into the drains.

The crowd watch uneasily while the mess is sluiced away. Soon it's all gone. The pavements are clean.

Bent to their tasks, avoiding eye contact with each other and the onlookers, the firemen hurry to roll up their hoses, pack up their gear and clamber aboard the fire engine. It rumbles away. It arrived looking big and red and impressive. It leaves looking big and red and somehow cowed, its tail between its legs, like a dog slinking out of the living room after shitting on the carpet.

I watch all this, numb, in a daze. My trouser legs and my hands are sticky with blood. I feel it dripping from my hair. It must be splashed all over my face.

The world is muted. Voices are a muzzy blur of incoherent sound. As I blink around me, I notice that everyone's staring. At me. No, not staring. They're shooting me looks as sharp and edgy as the bits of slate on the ground. Their mouths move, but I can't make out what they're saying, only the shapes of the words on their lips. Accusing ...

accusing me because I'm here, because I was there when the child was attacked in its pram, because I was there when the old ladies were attacked and when the beloved old angel was scared to death, and because I'm standing here now, all smeary with blood and bird shit and blurry in a halo of gulls . . .

The gulls are wild around my head. The blood and the gulls, that's why the people are staring at me. I stand in the middle of the square, an isolated bewildered figure, like someone bewitched, a mad and maddening and dangerous figure, so that people recoil from me and point and mouth strange accusing words.

As I turn away, I feel a spattering impact on my shoulders and on the back of my head. Instinctively I duck and swipe at my hair with my hands, thinking the gulls are splashing me with their droppings.

No, it's harder, more hurtful. Splinters of the slate that hit Brian. An old woman's bending to the ground for another handful. She flings them feebly at me. Her eyes are full of fear and anger, her lips squirm and show me her grey teeth, and she snarls at me, 'You . . . it's you.'

Another woman bends to the ground for something to throw. A child, with a white, frightened face, does the same. I hurry from the square.

NINETEEN

When my gull comes back, I'm downstairs in the yard with Pumpkin. I haven't been out much. I've got my bike upside down, oiling the chain and spinning the wheels by turning the pedals by hand. I'm thinking about my friend Brian Barltrop, who was damaged beyond repair by his visit to a very foreign country called Wales. He was transferred from Bangor Hospital to a special unit on the Wirral, not far from where he lived for most of his life. Home, back to the suburbs of England ... where, according to the article I read in the *North Wales Daily News,* 'he succumbed to his injuries' and went up in smoke in the crematorium at Ellesmere Port.

Succumbed. Brian would've liked that word. He would've reached for his dictionary, pushing aside a vase of privet and foxgloves, and looked it up. Nice word. Nice Brian.

And I'm thinking about me. How I've been for the past months, since Mum left and I hurt my hand: David Kewish, sulky and pouty and sarcastic, a grump, at odds with Kenny, at odds with the world. I think of something Dad said in one of his mind-numbing English lessons. We were 'doing' a story. In between the sighing and the muffled yawning, as he meandered around and around a familiar theme, he said that the main character in any story has got to be 'sympathetic', to be 'likable' or 'appealing' in some way, so that the reader'll be 'on his side' and want him to 'achieve his goals'. Something like that. And so I think of myself, and the challenges I've been given, and I wonder if anyone watching the way I'm handling them would like *me* at all, would care about *me,* my finger, my guitar, my moping about my absent mum and my passed-away dad.

I spin the wheels of my bike. The spokes shimmer in the sunlight. The chain runs smoothly, purring as though it's swallowed the oil I've given it and it's licking its lips like a contented kitten.

I think of Mum, and I blame her for making me so unappealing and unsympathetic. All right, so she's 'doing good' in Africa, she's wielding her shiny little first-aid kit of tweezers and scissors and needles and thread and sewing up stitches in ghastly wounds. But it would've been nice if she'd been here for *me,* for *my* wound and stitches, here for my birthday. Not just nice ... it would've changed everything. Kenny, a sneaky smoker when she's around, wouldn't have sent me out for cigarettes in the first place, he wouldn't have shouted after me, as I was turning out of the front door and into the street, those careless, matter-of-fact words . . . 'and a lighter, get me a lighter, will you?' and come blundering down the stairs like a fucking pisshead. So I blame her for the finger as well.

What would my dad ask the class now, if, hypothetically, he's still alive and we're all back in school again, reading *this* story? Putting a sharp little edge on his voice to stop us from wriggling in our seats, he might ask us about David Kewish: do we like him? is he a sympathetic character? Do we want him to achieve his goals?

Pete Shaw would sneer. 'I can't work out what his goals are, and I don't really give a toss. He's just a sulky twat feeling sorry for himself 'cos he's squashed his finger and can't play the guitar.'

Simon Reece would say, his spots reddening as everyone turns to look at him, 'I kind of know where he's coming from. His goals? He wants to get rid of Kenny, I don't know how and he doesn't know how . . . he wants his Mum to come back, and in the meantime he gets a bit of motherly comfort from the old gay guy Brian . . . and he's haunted by memories of his real Dad, who's somewhere in the bottom of the quarry, and he dreams of having him back too, but not in a grisly *Monkey's Paw* sort of way of course . . .' Simon shrugs. 'Yeah, I kind of like him, but he's got to grow up and stop sulking and tackle the challenges on his own.'

I let the wheels of the bike slow down and stop. A couple of times I have to push Pumpkin out of the way as she tries to put her nose to the spinning spokes. Now, as soon as the wheels stop turning, she comes waddling forward and nuzzles at my hands and sniffs at the oil. She sneezes so hard that her fat little body jumps into the air for a second. I pick her up and hold her very close. She smells lovely. Her coat's gleaming white, her nose a shiny black snub. Her teeth are perfect, her tongue's pink and sweet. In my arms, she's a puppy hot water bottle.

'Hey Pumpkin,' I whisper into her ear. 'You love me, don't you? Don't you?'

By way of response, she squirms away, crosses to the bike and pisses on the saddle. Nice one. Et tu, little brute. Then she throws a funny glance up into the sky. For a second, her eyeballs roll back and show white, and she hurries into the kitchen.

I look up too. There's a rummaging commotion in the ivy on top of the town wall, like a cat's caught a pigeon and is choking its windpipe, throttling a life away. The ivy's swaying and swishing . . .

But no. No cat. There's a flurry of brown feathers. A wheezy whistling cry, and a tremendous clatter of big, young, clumsy wings.

I jump up and run into the house. I know I've left my bedroom window wide open . . .

The gull's in the guitar case. When I run upstairs and into my room it's sitting there, as though it never left, poking the tattered old strip of my bloodstained bandage under its tummy, repairing its nest, picking at its own droppings which have crusted into the velvet. It cocks its head at me as I stand in the doorway. As if to say, yes I'm back, of course I'm back, and a tiny flicker of accusation in its eyes as though it's hurt and upset that I lured it out of town and dumped it there . . .

Hurt? I sit on the bed and lean closer to have a look. The bird's silent, just goggling at me, no cries, no peevish whistling like all the baby gulls in town. Not quite silent. There's a weird, wheezy sound, in time with the pulsing of its body. It's panting, a curious weedy panting like an old man struggling for breath.

'What's up? Hey, you're skinny. Didn't your mum look after you? What about the chip shop in Felinheli, and the pizza shop? Didn't you find any scraps there?'

The gull's big, yes, it sprawls its wings on either side of the guitar case, and they're big, like the mottled wings of a buzzard or even an eagle. But its body is thinner, not at all the plump well-fed chicken it was before I tried to get rid of it. 'Hey, what's up?' I ask again, and it allows my face closer and closer until my nose is almost touching its beak. 'Is that's why you've come back again? You're hungry and you think I'm going to feed you . . . is that it?'

But it doesn't make sense. I've never fed it. A sliver of bacon, maybe. And what's the sorry piping sound it's making? It lifts its beak towards me, opens wide and points the sharp little tongue. It breathes an indescribable breath into my face. Indescribable? Yes, and wonderful, the breath of a black-backed gull . . . the living breath of a wild sea-bird, with all the oceans of the world just waiting out there for it to beat its wings and go.

'What've you done? Let me see . . .'

The beak is damaged. The bird allows me to take hold of the tip with my fingers and angle it from side to side, and I can see that the lower jaw—the lower mandible, as Kenny would say in his super-knowledgeable professor's voice—is broken. A fragment of the beak is missing. There's a hole, and every time the bird breathes out it makes a faint, keen whistle.

'Poor little boy,' I whisper. 'Poor little girl. Whatever you are. Don't look at me like that. You mean it was me? *I* did it?'

Of course. As I let go of the beak and shift back onto my bed, as I look at the gull and it looks at me, I remember that horrible *clack-clack-clack*-ing . . . the bird with its beak caught in the spokes of my bike, the somersaulting, cartwheeling of its body and wings as I'd tried to get away, as I accelerated along the cycle track from Felinheli. I did it?

'So this is weird ... So you came to me, you pecked at my blood on the door, and you came to me and I took off the ring-pull ... I saved your life, all right? You took off my bandage, you showed me my stump. You pecked off the scab and you ate it ... right? And now you're back 'cos I broke your beak. What do you want me to do about it? Well?'

The ring-pull. I pull open my bedside drawer and look inside. There's a glint of silver among all the other odds and ends I've dumped inside. But before I can rummage around and find the gleam of aluminium I know is there somewhere, there's a buffeting of air, and in one single beat of its wings the gull lifts itself out of the guitar case and onto my bed ... Before I can blink, it's got its head into the drawer, its beak banging into the clutter ... its wings outspread, shadowing its prey, keeping me out, as though it's claiming some grisly prize it's found on the beach.

'Hey, do you mind? This is my room. These are my things ...'

It starts tossing everything out of the drawer. Fascinated, amused by what it's doing, I lie back and watch. There's a big bird in my room, on my bed, and I don't really mind because it's already made a very comfortable nest in my guitar case, and now it's into my bedside drawer and flicking things out, over one shoulder, over the other shoulder, its great brown wings mantling its prey, like a vulture plucking the guts from the belly of a dead zebra.

Until it finds what it wants.

The gull folds its wings and hops onto the floor again. It waddles very solemnly across the carpet and settles down into the guitar case. In its beak, in its broken beak, it's holding the red plectrum.

A piece of bright red plastic.

And get me a lighter, will you? The words flicker through my head. Not sure why. I see the bird with the splash of red in its beak and I hear those words, flickering through my head like lightning, burning and scalding the words onto my brain.

I run down to the living room. It's almost as if the bird's suggested it, planted the idea in my head. Kenny's out, and Pumpkin is quaking behind the sofa, knowing from the scent or the sounds from up in my room that the bird is back. I bump and barge around, fumbling into the sofa cushions, under newspapers and magazines and the directories by the telephone, until my fingers fold onto a lighter. I roll the wheel under my thumb, and the rough edges feel good, a pressure almost like pain. It flicks into life, first time, the flame very tall and straight. I hold it in front of my face and follow it up and up the stairs again . . . in and out of Kenny's fetid room for the Hendrix photo . . . back up to my bedroom . . .

Where the gull's waiting for me.

It's standing on my bed, its wide webbed feet sunk into the softness of my pillow, and it's holding the plectrum in its beak.

I sit on the bed. Very calm, as calm as the bird which is entranced by the flame I sway in front of its eyes, I take hold of the plectrum with the fingers of my other hand and tease it away.

'Give it to me . . . Let me have it . . . Good boy . . .'

I unroll the elastic bands from the photo and it springs open on my lap: a man kneeling to his blazing guitar, his hands raised as in prayer, the flames flickering at his fingers. A lovely sepia tone, the smears of dried piss.

I hold the plectrum over the image and apply the lighter to it.

For a few moments, nothing much happens. First there's a smell of hot plastic. The yellow flame turns blue, licking and sipping at the thing I'm holding gingerly in my fingers. And then, slowly, the plectrum starts to warp and fold, to change its shape in the magic of the fire. I drop the lighter, because the wheel under my thumb is burning hot, and I drop the plectrum too . . . not a plectrum anymore, but a blob of red stuff, which sizzles on the laminated photo.

For a miraculous second, a real flame rises from the flames in the picture . . . it straightaway dies, and sends a stink of smoke into the air.

The gull watches, as though in a trance, mesmerised by the brightness of the fire and the fume of the burning. It cocks its head from side to side, angling its eyes at the blob, at the puff of smoke, at my hands, at the spell I'm performing.

'Is it right?' I whisper. 'Am I doing it right?'

I pick up the plastic. It's hot, soft, and I roll it into a ball between my right thumb and forefinger. Too big. I tear it into two smaller pieces, careful to avoid its heat with the tender tip of my stump, drop one of the pieces, and work the other into a smooth flat sliver. And at the just the right moment, when the sliver is cooling and hardening and it's a dull red pill on the palm of my hand, the gull dips its head forward and touches it with its beak.

I hold the bird with my left hand—yes, the very first thing that I deliberately touch with my stump is the beak of a black-backed gull. I squeeze hard enough to keep the bird still, until I can feel the soreness of my soft new skin, and with my right fingers I apply the plastic to the broken place on the beak.

A quick squeeze. Another dab, to make sure it's in place. A final smear, to mould it into the jagged edges where the beak is cracked. Done.

I let go of the gull. It recoils from me and from the smell of the molten plastic. It springs off the bed and onto the guitar case on the floor, where it folds its wings and plumps itself down, snuggling its breast into the velvet.

'There. Like magic.'

The bird opens its beak wide, yawns, and hisses and clacks its jaws like castanets. And when it settles into its nest, breathing slowly and evenly, there's no more wheezing. It closes its eyes, drops its head onto its breast, and falls asleep.

TWENTY

And so the bird resumes its old routine.

It comes and goes as it wants, into my room from the town wall, out of the window and disappearing for hours on end whenever it feels like it. I still don't feed it. It quickly bulks up again, waddling around the streets among all the juvenile herring gulls, swaggering and bullying through them because of its bigger size and greater weight and getting the best scraps. Only the day after it returned, it's been out and about and come back absolutely bursting, its tummy round and fat, full of chips and bread crusts and whatever else it's gorged on.

Big bird. Big appetite. Eat anything. Eat everything.

I don't tell Kenny the gull is back. He doesn't know it was gone in the first place, because I haven't told him about my cycle ride to Felinheli and my treacherous attempt to dump it. From the balcony of the Queen's Gate, a grandstand view, he watched the horrible nonsense of the firemen trying to shift the gulls' nests from the rooftops and then the fall of the slate. He saw how people reacted to me after the accident. He could've said he told me so ... because, way back, he warned me about having the baby gull following me around the streets of the town. But now he thinks it's gone forever, and the whole topic of my connection with the gulls is an uneasy taboo.

We never mention it. And I hardly go out.

The gull still comes to the house, to my room. Whenever Kenny trudges upstairs to bring me a cup of tea or to be nosey about what I'm doing up here, it hears him and flaps up to the window and out. I've started to burn joss sticks to disguise the fishy smell that the gull brings with it, so in the privacy of my own almost-private space, overlooking the street on one side and the ivy-covered wall on the other, the air has soaked up the typical fusty-mustiness of a teenage boy's bedroom . . . the boy-smell of body and bed and hair and clothes, sometimes deodorant, usually not.

And another smell. Something in the wardrobe.

'I kind of like it, actually,' Kenny admits, glancing around and sniffing. He's come upstairs one afternoon to see what I'm up to. 'Your mum wouldn't, but it reminds me of a bed-sit I had in Bangor a few years ago, kind of homely, the joss sticks, you know, your own stuff.' He inhales long and noisily through his beaky nose. 'And something else . . . What is it?'

I don't answer. He has no idea. He won't believe me if I tell him. I've had all Dad's clothes washed and dry-cleaned. But, despite my efforts with the guitar, using bleach and different kinds of disinfectant, it's terminally impregnated with Kenny's piss. It was impossible to drain everything out of it; however I turned it and shook it and tried to spill it out, there was no way I could get every drop. I sprayed inside it. I dribbled in bleach. I stood it in the sunlight from my window and when I thought it was dry I dropped in a handful of lavender potpourri.

No good. The guitar stinks. A curiously animal odour of varnish, glue, wood, and urine. And it's getting stronger. The guitar seems to be sucking it all in, all the residual moisture and its unique pungency, into the curves of the body and up and up, by some kind of capillary reaction, into its neck.

The heat too. It's been sweltering for days, for the past week. Into the second half of August, the peak of the tourist season and the height of a hot summer, the temperature has risen and stayed high day and night. Some people are cranky about it. Sleepless at night, bad-tempered in the daytime, tourists and locals alike are moaning about the airlessness, the suffocating stillness of the air . . . wishing for a bit of a breeze or a shower of rain. Others, of course, instead of complaining because the summer's so hot and the skies so clear and blue, are rubbing their hands happily as the money rolls in . . . the pubs are busy, the visitors are queuing for ice creams and cold drinks.

'Talking of Mum,' I put in, to try and catch Kenny before he changes the subject again, 'have you heard from her, if she's coming back?'

He looks sideways at me, cocky and quizzical like a jackdaw, and then glances into the wardrobe mirror to inspect the grey stubble on his chin. Trying not to be sarcastic, I persist. 'Hey Kenny, you mentioned Mum just then. I know you didn't mean to, it just slipped out because of the weird smell in my bedroom, but you mentioned her and I was wondering if . . .'

'She's still on her Florence Nightingale trip, you know that, David. Nothing's changed.' To avoid looking at me, he lifts his chin a few more degrees and studies the hairs in his nostrils as if they're incredibly fascinating. 'She'll be back when she wants to come back, or when the pirates realise they ain't getting their ransom and they kick her out of the harem. Can't we just let the rest of the summer pan out? This is the busiest time of the season, my tours and everything. In a week or two it'll be September and the end of the holidays and back-to-school and all that, so in the meantime I'm . . .'

'And what are you going to do in September, Kenny? When there are no more tourists? In the autumn and the winter, when it's pissing rain and pitch-dark at four o'clock in the afternoon? How many customers will you have on your spooky tours then? What are you going to do?'

Cornered, he raises his eyebrows at me. 'Hey, Mr land-owner, Mr landed gentry, don't niggle me. What's the big deal about me doing something I like doing and making a bit of pocket money out of it? Your mum goes all Lady Di and tootling off to *save the children,* you get the hump and spend the holiday sulking in your bedroom . . .'

He sees me opening my mouth and guesses what I'm going to say. Holding up his hands in the familiar don't-shoot-me attitude, he adds quickly, 'No, Dave, no. Don't go on about your finger. It was an accident. I'm sorry, all right? Nothing to do with your mum for running away and leaving you. An accident, all right?'

I gape at him. The words come out. 'A lighter . . . get me a lighter, will you?'

'What?'

'Don't you remember, Kenny? That's what you shouted to me. I heard you shouting something, so I turned round and put my finger into the hinge of the door. You slammed the door shut.'

He's staring at me.

'Remember? And then you scraped the squashed bit of my finger out of the door and put it in an envelope and gave it to the doctor. A bit too late, because it was squashed.'

I lean to my bedside table, snatch something off it. 'Here, Kenny . . . I got it.'

I toss a lighter through the air towards him. It spins through the dusty sunlight, a gleam of plastic and metal and a capsule of fuel, a miniature spaceship. I think he's going to catch it. But he doesn't. He just stands there, without moving, and lets it hit him on the chest and drop to the floor.

Ignoring it and ignoring me, he shuffles to the door and goes downstairs.

TWENTY-ONE

Hot. And it gets hotter.

A wearisome time for some people, red-faced and irritable, huffing and puffing and complaining of sleepless nights and headaches and the noise of the gulls screaming around the rooftops at two and three o'clock in the morning. A busy time for others, in the business of feeding and watering the tourists, making as much money as they can in just a few hectic weeks.

It's getting to me too. Monday morning, and I've been lying late in bed—windows wide open, as always—listening to the sounds of the town outside. Jangly, jarring noises: people shouting, cars hooting on the nearby square, music from a neighbour's radio or the pub across the street. The gulls. All through the night they've been squalling and yelling and bawling and hurtling over the rooftops. Nonstop. Late in the summer, now that all of their chicks have hopped out of the nests and slithered down to the pavements, the gulls are on the move, on an endless, twenty-four-hour, day-and-night search for scraps wherever they can find them.

Roosting? Resting? Sleeping? No, they don't have time for any of that. The pesky chicks are always hungry, demanding more and more to guzzle into their bulging bellies. Won't they ever be satisfied? Won't they ever give up asking for more? No, life for the gulls in the castle towers and medieval town of Caernarfon is a whirlwind of wings and beaks . . . and a mad, never-ending noise.

This morning, I'm in the category of headachy moaners myself. I've slept so badly that my single sheet's twisted into a shapeless bundle I've kicked off the bed and onto the floor. I mooch down to the kitchen to gulp a glass of water. Kenny's gone out—probably already halfway through his first castle tour of the day. To let a bit more air through the house, he's left the door open onto Hole in the Wall Street, chocked with a stopper so it can't bang shut. I make myself a mug of coffee and head back upstairs.

'Hey, Pumpkin . . .' In the living room, she's snoozing on the sofa, among a jumble of magazines that Kenny's left there. She opens one eye and groans as she hears me padding past her.

'Hey, my little puppy . . . come on, my sleepy pup.' With my free hand, the mug of coffee in the other, I hoick her off the sofa and hold her against my tummy. 'You're hot as a pie . . .'

She squirms a bit as I start up to my room. She hasn't been there for weeks. 'It's all right. I won't let anything hurt you. It's just you and me . . .'

Upstairs, I plop her onto the bedroom floor. She sniffs around for a while, checking under the bed and in all the corners, sneezing disgustedly at the encrusted guitar case. At last she seems satisfied that I've told her the truth. She curls up on my sweaty bed sheet, snuffling her face into it as though it's the most delicious thing she's ever smelt, and she's asleep a second later.

I sprawl on the bed with my mug of coffee. The sounds of the town fade from my hearing, become a comforting blur. Each sip of coffee is clearing the muzziness of my head, the room seems a bit cooler, and I can see the dog's fat, white tummy going up and down with every breath.

A noise from inside the wardrobe. A ping. And a groan.

I lie on my bed, hot, bored, muzzy. I grope for my coffee, on my bedside table. There's another groan from inside the wardrobe, a longer creaking and then a quick soft pop.

I put down my coffee and get up, nudged out of my haze of laziness, and I grope blindly into the wardrobe.

The stink hits me. The guitar's leaning in the corner of its horrid suffocating prison. And it's breaking. A prisoner in solitary confinement, beaten by the darkness and loneliness and injustice, it's breaking itself.

I snatch it out and cross to my bed with it. The neck's burst upwards from the body. The tension of the strings, increased hour by hour and day by day from the heat in the wardrobe and the absorbed dampness of urine, has snapped the base of the neck up and out of the rounded shoulders of the body of the guitar.

Too late, too late . . . hissing at myself in anger and frustration, I turn and turn the machine heads to loosen the strings. Too late. The guitar's pulled itself apart. Wracked by the moisture in all its joints, it must've ached and ached until the ache was too much to endure . . . too much to bear, the seepage of piss into every grain of the wood, so that the joints swelled and cracked and finally splintered. I loosen the strings until they flap. Too late.

What to do? Cry? Or wail? Or just grind my teeth? I hold the guitar on my knee, my left hand to the frets and my right hand to the strings, as though I'm going to play it. But two things are wrong. On my left hand, the stump of my forefinger sticks up and out and goes nowhere near the frets. And the long graceful neck of the guitar is bent from the lovely curvy body at an unnatural angle, as though someone's twisted and snapped it. Killed it.

Lovely . . . yes, it's still lovely, despite the smell of it and its deadly uselessness. I feel the anger slip away from me. Idly I thrum at the flabby strings, and the discord is jangly, strangely in tune with the morning.

Through it, I hear another sound from outside. A familiar sound of the long, thirsty summer . . . a warning *peep-peep-peep,* the rumble of an engine, as a lorry reverses down the street and stops below my window. Beer, more beer. The brewery is delivering to the Goron Fach, the pub just opposite our front door.

I thrum the chord. The whole room seems to hum with it. At the same time, with my left hand I unwind the bass string more and more and tug it out of the machine head. It coils like a living thing, slithering in my fingers until I feed it through the hole in the bridge of the guitar and it's completely free. And then it lies flaccid on the bed, perfectly straight the whole of its length, with a tight hard coil at the end where it's been wound into the machine head. From outside my window a beat begins, a heavy, rhythmic thud, and I know what it is, without looking . . . The brewery men are unloading the barrels; one after another, one man dropping a barrel off the back of the lorry and onto a padded mat, another man steadying it and rumbling it down into the cellar of the pub . . . *Thud, thud, thud* . . .

I thrum the chord to the beat of the barrels. The room goes dark. A shadow fills the window and the day is blotted out.

Is it the chord? Hypnotic, the oddness of the notes and the pulse of the rhythm? Is it the chord that summons the black-back?

The gull's at the window, spreading its wings like a cloak. With a clacking of its beak, as if to show off the splash of red on its lower jaw, it launches itself into the room and lands with a clumsy, sprawling impact beside me on the bed.

'Pumpkin! Get away! Get away from it!'

The dog's on her feet and yapping. She leaps at the bird, and her needle-sharp puppy-teeth go for the throat. I try to grab her off, but she snarls horribly at me, wrinkling her muzzle like a stoat, and the bird thrashes at me with its wings.

'Pumpkin! Get off it!'

They're up for it, both of them. They don't want me to interfere. I jump up and away from the bed.

The gull's big and heavy. Something in the weight of its wings and the stabbing, the jabbing of its beak drives the dog away. The bird makes itself huge, it seems to inflate itself, to bulk itself up by standing tall and slapping its feet and swaggering with its wings held high. It storms at the dog, forcing her back and back to the edge of the bed, banging the grey metallic beak into the snarling puppy-face.

It all happens in a moment. Pumpkin's on the brink. The gull senses the advantage. It wades forward, hissing, sticking out the thin sharp tongue, and a second later the puppy has no space left. She squirms away and rolls backwards onto the floor. She dives headlong down the stairs.

I watch from the open door of the wardrobe. The whole thing, in less than half a minute, is reflected haphazardly in the mirror. I expect the gull to shuffle its wings and flap up to the window and out again ... but no. It leaps after the dog. For a bizarre moment it stalls in mid-air, as though dangling by some invisible thread ... There's a gleam of silver and I see the guitar string snagged round its foot. It beats and beats the mighty young wings, tugs the string away from the bedclothes and springs downstairs in pursuit of the puppy, trailing the string behind it.

I follow. I reach the living room in time to see the gull driving the puppy from behind the sofa. Again I lunge forward to try and grab the dog and pick her up, but I miss, stumbling to my knees, jabbing my stump painfully onto the floor. Pumpkin flees to the door. Again she disappears downstairs, plunging for safety in the bottom of the house.

The bird's right behind her. I'm right behind the bird. I try to halt it by stamping on the guitar string, but miss and miss ...

The puppy sees the open front door. She's out, in a

streak of terrified white fur. The gull yelps, an ugly rasping cry of triumph, and springs after her. Into the street.

Thud. Thud. The beer barrels keep on their steady pulsing rhythm.

I reach the door. The puppy, running blind, is a flash of white. She runs for the lorry, to dive underneath it. The barrel rolls off the lorry. It turns in mid-air, and the sun gleams on the bulge of metal.

A man shouts. Too late. The barrel lands with a thud and a high-pitched squeal.

TWENTY-TWO

'Dray,' Kenny says. 'I'm pretty sure that's the word. Strictly speaking, it's a dray.'

I blink at him in disbelief. We're sitting on the sofa in our living room. I'm trying to tell him what happened this morning. I've waited until he's come home for a sandwich at lunchtime, and I know he's got to go back into the castle for the two o'clock tour.

'No, Kenny, don't just make everything up, like you do with the tourists. People don't use horses and carts anymore, except maybe in Egypt and Afghanistan and places like that. They may have called it a dray in Victorian times, but nowadays a brewery delivers barrels of beer to a pub in a thing called a truck. It was a truck, all right? I saw it with my own eyes. Now can I tell you the rest of the story?'

Kenny shrugs at me and steals a furtive glance at his watch. He's more concerned about getting back to the castle on time than about listening to what I'm trying to tell him.

'To cut it short then . . . they were delivering beer to the Goron Fach . . . and Pumpkin shot out of the front door and into the street ... you left the door open, didn't you, when you went out this morning?'

'So it's my fault, is it? Is that the point you're making? It's always my fault, isn't it?'

'I didn't say it was your fault, Kenny. Except that it wouldn't have happened if you hadn't left the door open, all right? That's all I'm saying. Can I finish?'

He stuffs the last piece of his sandwich into his mouth. He doesn't chew it. He takes a swig of his tea, and then he chews. He makes a disgusting sloppy sound, mulching the bread and cheese and tea together, and then he swallows it all down.

'She shot out of the front door and straight for the lorry. I couldn't do anything. I just watched. The barrel rolled off the lorry and she was right underneath it ...'

I pause. An image of that moment burns so hot inside my head that I can't find the words to describe it. The little white dog in a suicide dash for the exact spot where the barrel will drop ... the gleam of the sun on the barrel ... the man on the lorry who glimpses her and shouts a warning ... the man on the ground, waiting by the mat to steady the barrel when it lands.

I hear the sickening thud. I hear the squeal.

'She was right underneath it. The guy heard his mate shout, he spotted Pumpkin ... He stuck out his foot and knocked her out of the way. Just in time.'

Kenny wipes his mouth with the back of his hand. He stands up and looks at his watch again. 'A lucky escape,' he says. 'Hey Pumpkin, we're talking about you, by the way.' He leans down and pats her soft pink tummy. She's lying flat on her back, fast asleep on the mess of newspapers on the sofa. 'A lucky escape, hey Pumpkin?'

'Not so lucky for the guy who kicked her out of the way,' I say. 'The barrel landed right on his foot. Broke all his toes. You should've heard him squeal.'

Kenny hurries downstairs. I hear him in the kitchen, rinsing his teeth at the sink. As he leaves the house, he shouts up to me, 'I'm shutting the door, all right? Can you keep the dog inside this afternoon? I mean, are we going to get sued by the brewery or something?'

The door closes and I hear his footsteps as he goes up the street towards the castle.

I haven't mentioned the gull. I haven't told him the gull was in the house, the real reason why Pumpkin fled outside. There was a noisy commotion after the barrel crushed the man's foot. One squeal, and then, rolling on the pavement, he grits his teeth and manages to express his pain in a more manly groaning. Pumpkin starts licking his face, either to stop the ugly noise or because she's sorry for the trouble she's causing . . . eager to smuggle her out of the way as quickly as possible, I pick her up, tumble her back into the house, and shut the door. And then the landlord, looking sideways at me in an odd way, as though remembering a similar incident I was involved in earlier in the summer, helps the injured man into the back of his car and takes him off to the hospital.

The gull? It springs away, up the street, making huge leaps with its wings spread wide. Tourists step aside to let it go by. A young woman with a pushchair swerves and stops and crouches over her child as though a bomb's about to go off. The gull disappears. I hear a hoarse, distant cackling, and when I look up I see the parent bird circling and circling high up. The black-back is watching. It's seen everything.

Now I'm alone again in the house, with the sleeping puppy. She's lying with her legs splayed out, her tummy like pink satin with her tiny nipples sticking up. Her eyes are tight shut, but the lids are twitching rapidly.

'What are you dreaming about, hey Pumpkin? A big monster crashing through the window and attacking you?

It isn't fair, is it? When I found you, a whole lot of nasty birds were trying to peck you to death, and now a monster's jumping through the window and chasing you into the street.'

She's miles away, worlds away. I leave her fast asleep on the sofa and go back up to my room.

What was I doing? I look around, trying to see everything for the first time, like a policeman surveying the scene of a murder. A mug of coffee on the bedside table, half empty, the surface scummy and cold. The guitar case, plush velvet with a lot of greeny-yellow stains. Window flung wide, skylight open. Wardrobe door, wide open. The bed unmade . . . and lying on it, there's a shapely naked body, with a broken neck.

I pick up the five-stringed guitar, all the time watching myself in the wardrobe mirror: an eighteen-year-old youth, his lips pursed, his hair tousled, his face still bleary from a lazy lie-in . . . his eyes somehow disappointed, anxious, afraid . . .

I see fear in my own face. And the words come out of my mouth. 'It makes you wonder who's going to be next?'

I strum once on the guitar. As soon as I hear the eerie chord that brought the gull back into the house, as I glance nervously toward the open window, I damp it straightaway with the palm of my hand. I feel for the machine heads. With a sense of calm and certainty I haven't experienced for weeks, I continue to do what I was doing when the bird interrupted me . . .

I unwind the remaining strings. In a few moments, I've undone them from the machine heads and unplugged them from the belly of the guitar as well.

And then, for the first time since my birthday, I put the guitar back into its case. I lay it gently inside its comfortably lined coffin. I curl up the five strings and press them into the silvery-grey velvet, as though they're precious artefacts to take into the afterlife. I zip up the case. At last I push it far into the back of the wardrobe, into the deepest darkness, where it's completely hidden behind all of Dad's clothes.

It's silent. It doesn't have a voice. It's broken and dead and done with. I close and lock the door.

TWENTY-THREE

'It's going to be mad! August Bank Holiday, the last week-end of the season! It'll be mad, through Friday, Saturday, Sunday, right up to the big climax on Monday. The carnival! Did I tell you there's a carnival on Monday?'

So the summer's drawing to a close. Hot sun and blue skies. The town's bright and noisy and full of visitors: coachloads from Manchester and Birmingham and Liverpool; different species of foreign tourists; cars queuing to get into the square and find somewhere to park along the quayside; stampedes of motorcycles on day trips from Llangollen and Chester.

Beer. Ice cream. Fish and chips. Seagulls and the smell of the sea.

The gift shops are packed, selling postcards and souvenirs. 'The Royal Borough of Caernarfon: a perfectly preserved thirteenth-century castle and walled town, the pinnacle of Edward I's conquest of Wales and the birthplace of his son, the first English Prince of Wales . . . more recently the scene of the Investitures of the modern Princes of Wales in 1911 and 1969.' I know all this from school, and from Kenny's tours. Caernarfon's only a little seaside town, drizzly and grim through the winter, but in the summer it shakes itself awake again, gets a lick of paint and dozens of hanging baskets overflowing with flowers, and reminds everyone that it's 'a World Heritage Site, as famous all over the world as the Taj Mahal or the Niagara Falls' . . .

'Yes Kenny, you told me about the carnival. Quite a few times already.'

He's really excited about it. The Monday's going to be special for him, for two reasons. First of all, the people who look after Caernarfon Castle—something called Cadw, part of the Welsh Office which runs all the historic sites in Wales—are sending a film crew from Cardiff to do a feature on the castle and the town in the throes of the holiday madness. They'll be shooting all around the town, inside the castle of course, and they've prepped Kenny to take the crew up and down a few towers, to do his party piece into the camera so they get some spectacular angles and the low-down on the castle's history. He's going to be famous. No, that's an exaggeration . . . He's going to be on Welsh television for about thirty seconds.

The other reason? He's been booked to do a spot onstage, at the carnival.

'Hey, don't be snidey about the air guitar,' he says, when he first starts crowing about it. We're standing in the kitchen one morning, with bacon sandwiches and mugs of coffee, and he's as excited as if he's a real musician going to play the Albert Hall or Madison Square Garden or somewhere like that. 'Don't start curling your lip and sneering about it,' he says, smearing at his own greasy mouth with the back of his hand. 'Air guitar is big. It's global. There's been a world championship for bloody years, since the first one in Finland back in 1996. It isn't just anybody arsing around with a tennis racquet, jumping up and down and doing stupid windmills with his arms and pulling stupid faces. It's . . .'

I make the mistake of looking interested. In fact, I've got a piece of very hot, fried bread stuck onto the roof of my mouth, so I can't interrupt him even if I want to.

'Haven't I told you about it before?' he goes on. 'There are strict rules and regulations for the competitions. You do a one-minute spot, no props, no nothing, just you and your air guitar, and you get points for three different things. First of all, there's technical merit, that's how much you look like you're really playing your chords, doing your fretwork. Then there's stage presence, your charisma, your star quality, your showmanship. And finally . . .' He hurries on, because he can see I've cleared my mouthful with a swig of coffee and might try to stop him. 'And finally, most importantly of all, there's a marvellous and mysterious thing known as airness.'

The fried bread's burnt my mouth. It's sore where I feel with the tip of my tongue.

'Airness . . .' He pauses and savours the word, with a far-away, dreamy smile on his face, as though the wondrousness of the concept has cast a spell on him. 'Do you know what it is, according to the regulations of the Air Guitar World Championships?' He takes a breath, closes his eyes and presses his hands together as if he's praying. 'Airness: the extent to which a performance transcends the imitation of a real guitar and becomes an art form in itself.'

Air guitar. An art form. It doesn't make me feel any better, about myself or about Kenny. I stare at his fingers. They're so long and perfectly manicured. All ten of them.

'Yes, Kenny,' I say. 'The carnival's going to be fun and I'm sure you'll be the star of the show.' I'm trying hard not to be too ungracious. 'It'll be fun, I've got the message.' I swill the dregs of my coffee into the sink. I throw the crusts of my greasy sandwich into the back yard.

I can feel it already, a dark hollow space in my belly. The end of the summer. The carnival signals the end of my messed-up summer. There's always a carnival in town, and so much fun that it makes me uneasy. Because the fun is so manic and overblown, it overwhelms and engulfs everyone in its bullying, compulsory way . . . You *have to* have fun, you *have to* . . . Hard to explain, but it gives me a sickly, churning feeling in the pit of my stomach. Because it's all going to end . . . when the carnival's over and all the visitors have gone and there's nothing but a dreary silence and left-overs—or hangovers, more likely—and the party's over.

Glum. I spin out of the kitchen. Kenny's calling after me, 'Hey don't be a grump! Wars will end and all bad things will go away, if everyone just plays air guitar. That's what it's all about! It's as simple as that! It isn't just a hobby or a game . . . It's a way of life!'

So the big day arrives. Bank Holiday Monday, a glorious mid-afternoon, and the party's reaching the climax that Kenny's been going on about.

I'm not there, of course. I'm moping in my room. But I can hear the thumping bass and drums of rock 'n' roll from the marquee by the castle. I'm probably the only person in Caernarfon who isn't there, apart from the geriatrics in their fetid old people's homes and the terminal patients festering in the cottage hospital.

Me and the very old. Me and the very sick. We're the only ones who aren't there.

Hey I'm doing a funny thing, an unusual thing for me. I just feel like it, I guess. On the way past Kenny's room, I pause and look in and inhale the fume of booze from the carpet and curtains and the yellowy bed sheets, and I spot the bottle under his bed. Dark rum. A half-empty bottle of coke too. Maybe it's the stink of the alcohol . . . or the feeling that everyone in the world's at it except me . . . I pick up both the bottles and bring them up to my room and mix them into my coffee mug. It's warm and flat and I think I've made it too strong. It tastes like cough medicine. So I gulp it down and it burns my throat and my chest and I try another one to see if it does the same. It does. I gulp it down and it does, it burns. It makes my eyes water.

And it feels nice. So now I'm onto my third mugful of rum and coke.

Thump thump thump. The drums and bass from the quayside . . . I'm all heaty with rum, so I pull off my shirt and lie back on my bed and close my eyes and feel the thumping in my chest. It's so loud it makes the wardrobe *buzz buzz buzz.* I sit up sharply and drain my mug, lean to the bottles on the floor, and slop in another dose of the medicine . . . not much coke left, so it's mostly rum and the smell's so strong I can smell it at arm's length as I swing the mug merrily closer and closer to my mouth and catch it on my lips with a long sweet wet kiss . . .

That's nice. And the *buzz buzz buzz* makes me wonder what's buzzing in the wardrobe. Can't be the guitar, which has no strings and is muffled away forever in its funereal body bag. I shimmy across the room, sway for a moment in front of the mirror, and smile lovingly at myself for being so tall and well made and the only teenager in town who doesn't need to be schmoozing at a boring old medieval party that's probably been going on the castle quayside since the end of the thirteenth century, and I tug the door open.

So what's buzzing? It's just a couple of coat hangers tingling together . . . hanging out, feeling the beat, tenderly tingling in the warm darkness. Not the guitar, of course. But I reach for it anyway, where I hid it away in the furthest corner, behind Dad's clothes. A warm mugful of rum and coke in my right hand, I press my left hand among his clothes and catch his scent and feel his caress on the soft swollen tip of my stump.

On impulse, I put on one of his shirts. I knot one of his mismatching colour-blind ties around my neck. I tug at his schoolteaching jacket and put it on. I can smell him, my father, a strangely familiar smell through the cough-mixture rum and the lingering ammonia of Kenny's piss.

Cheers, Dad. I look at him in the mirror and toast him. He raises his glass and smiles back. The strongness of the rum, or maybe the image of my father and the scent of him so warmly enfolding me . . . something makes my eyes tingle. Cheers. The coat hangers are still tingling too, to the beat of the bass and drums at the carnival. I feel for the guitar.

It isn't there.

My finger bangs on the back of the wardrobe. I grope downwards and find the case, collapsed into a heap. I yank it out. It's empty.

In another moment of confusion and bewilderment I toss it onto the floor and rummage inside it . . . I don't know why, as though I'm stupidly expecting somehow to find the guitar if I dig deeply enough. Nothing. Only the strings come spooling out, uncoiling themselves all over the floor and slithering together like a nest of snakes. And there's a piece of paper . . . some kind of a note, a scrawl of writing.

Clumsy black felt-tip. On the back of an old phone bill. *'Hey Dave, had a great idea, dont think your using this right now . . . can i use it for my gig?'*

The heat of the rum swarms through my body. I feel it like a flood of blood in my neck and colouring my face and boiling into the top of my head.

I form the words I can hear the words I mouth the words at myself in the mirror . . . So Kenny fucking Phelps . . . You can piss in my mother's wardrobe and all over her clothes so she fucks off to Africa . . . You can piss in my wardrobe and all over my dad's clothes and claim your fucking territory in this house and in my life . . . You can throw my bird—*my* bird!—out of the house and into the street and expect it'll never come back again . . . but you can't just feel your thieving kicking fingers into my stuff and take my guitar, the guitar I bought for myself and can never play for two fucking reasons—one 'cos you smashed my fucking finger in the door and two 'cos you pissed into the guitar so it's warped and broken and dead and so now you want to burn it in front of all your stupid fucking friends . . .

I sound drunk. I'm angry and the rum's hot inside me. It flurries me out of the room and flings me down the stairs and into the street.

Thump thump thump . . . The beat of the bass in Twll Yn Yr Wal. So the old and the sick can't be where it's at, but I hurry past the castle and onto the quayside, where the rest of the world's having a party . . . and I'm shoving my way into the crowd.

Hundreds of people in different degrees of party mood, from red-faced and mellow to totally rat-arsed . . . to use one of Kenny's favourite expressions and one of Mum's least favourite. And, as angry as I am, or was when I first found that Kenny'd filched the guitar for a little bonfire to enliven his airness, I feel a flush of exhilaration too. Easy, hey it's easy, to pick up a drink here or there . . . There's horrid plastic glasses of warm soapy beer just lying around and dregs of cheap red wine and sometimes a leftover slug of rum or gin or something else that's fiery and flushes my face and fuels the fierce place in the top of my head . . . So I'm weaving among the jostle and sway of the carnival in a muzzy-headed maddened way, with a glass of this or that in each hand.

Hot . . . Noisy . . . Beer everywhere, splashed and spilled in a reckless wanton way and a lot more being guzzled down a thousand thirsty throats . . .

I stand in the middle of the mass of people, feel the sun on my head and the glow of it on my beery-boy's face, and I repeat the phrase inside my head. A thousand thirsty throats . . . I try it again and again, louder and louder, until I blink and look around and see a circle of reddened faces gawping at me and I realise I'm saying it aloud: 'a thousand thirsty throats!' And I raise my drinks stupidly in the air. The faces laugh at me with wet blurry lips, and then they—and no doubt the heads and bodies to which they're attached—blur a bit more and move away, until the crowd's a busy blur again.

No, I'm not drunk. Well, no drunker than anybody else. So yes, a little bit hazy on a cocktail of slurps and dregs and foam. I don't like the tastes . . . a sickly syrup on my tongue and lining my throat and I feel the anger with Kenny slipping out of focus . . . I hang onto one of the drinks . . . could be lager or something, it looks like piss and it's warm and it reminds me of Kenny and . . . I hang onto the glass in case I bump into a school friend and need to look cool, but when I find myself close to the edge of the quay I accidentally-on-purpose slop most of the beer out of it. It spatters on the deck of a yacht which is moored there, onto the perfectly white back of a swan cruising for scraps. Leaning over the water—the deep dark greenness of it and the way the beads of beer roll through the plumage—for a moment I find a private space in a crazy world . . . and I know I don't need the beer at all, not even the scum in the bottom of the glass to try and impress my friends.

A few long deep breaths. I pour it all away, careful to miss the swan, and push my way back into the crowd.

Music too . . . against the beetling walls of the castle there's a brilliantly stripy marquee, white and orange stripes, like a circus tent. And the best music coming from inside. A guitar band, rhythm and blues, a lazy thumping rock 'n' roll . . . a bumping bass guitar, super-tight drums, and the sweetest guitar singing the blues in its mellowest summer-holiday mood. I push through. No, I burrow through . . . No, I'm absorbed through the crowd because the music's got me on a hook and line and's reeling me in, closer and closer. Until I get to the marquee and squeeze my way inside.

And there I'm lost for a while. Sober. Calming. The anger draining away . . .

A middle-aged man, so cool it doesn't matter if he's six-teen or ninety-six, is playing the blues ... and then rhythm and blues and rock 'n' roll, so slick and swaggering it makes the canvas quiver. A super three-piece band ... a guitarist I almost recognise from the archive photos in my music magazines, who played clubs all over the world while I was at kindergarten ...

A lot of smoke. A lot of beer. The band on a makeshift stage. Straw underfoot. Hay bales buttressed against the wall of the castle and stacked up for people to sit on, to sprawl on, to stand on and dance on, to spill their beer on. What more do you want? Simply the music. I perch on the edge of a bale and listen, and the beat buzzes through my body, throbbing to the very tip of the stump of my finger.

But then there's Kenny. And my anger comes back.

While the real guitarist's playing, Kenny's aping with his air guitar. He's lurking at the back of the stage, warming up for his big moment ... doing slithery little moves with his hips and goofing in thin air with an imaginary guitar. Where did he learn those faces, the grimaces and sneers, as though he's mastering a real guitar and wringing the music from it? Where did he learn those chords, the way he shapes them so beautifully with the long strong fingers of his left hand? How did he learn that finger work, so smooth and slick and stroking the strings so sweetly? He didn't! He didn't! He's just aping them, babooning and chimping and insulting all the hours of work and practice and all the talent of the real musician he's aping ...

He sees me. He waves at me. He has the gumption to look embarrassed. And sorry. He reaches down for some-thing and straightens up. He's got my guitar in one hand, a bottle of lighter fluid in the other, and an appealing look on his face. Can I? he's asking. Can I? Please?

A bubble of anger bursts inside my head. Rum and rock 'n' roll and I'm lunging for the stage ...

All around me, their faces swollen and sweaty and gawping into mine, the crowd's a huge live thing, a swirling and hotly breathing creature. I'm shoving against it, into it, and my vision's reddened by the rum and the noise and the overwhelming need to get at Kenny fucking Phelps . . .

Hey Mr Kewish sir! Voices, like a long-ago echo from long-ago years . . . a name, my name, no not my name but Kewish hey Kewish, Mr Kewish sir . . . I wheel around wildly to see where they're coming from. It's Simon and the others from my class, faces from schooldays and Dad's classroom, and suddenly they're grinning and brawling around me and yanking at my tie and yanking at my jacket, the tie and jacket I'd forgotten I was wearing, and they're rummaging at me and rumpling me and bullying me away from the stage and through the madly crowd and out of the marquee into the beery hot sunshine.

It's Simon Reece and Pete Shaw, with their guitars. And a mob of other boys and girls from school, some I liked and some I didn't.

'Hey sir! It's Mr Kewish sir! How you doing Mr Kewish sir?' they're yelling with their hands in my pockets and straightening my tie too tight into a hard, hard knot on my throat.

'Hey Simon hey Pete . . .' I'm mumbling back at them, my tongue too big and clumsy in my mouth, my eyes on their guitars and their fuzzy faces . . . 'Hey the music's fantastic! You been in the marquee?'

They've all got beer. The girls too. They raise their glasses towards me, slosh a spatter of foam at my face and into my hair. Simon angles his guitar at me like a rifle, as though he's pulling the trigger on me . . . Pete Shaw too, jabbing his guitar like a bayonet, and yes he's left-handed but he looks kind of cool.

And I surprise myself. No envy. No bitterness. I just stand there and beam at them, ambushed by the glow I'm feeling to be back with my friends, in a flood of relief that my meany mood is melting away. Hey, I'm the centre of attention . . . me and my finger.

The girls are all over me. Tricia Turton, who I never liked and always needled me for being Daddy's boy and teacher's pet, she's holding my hand and making ugh-gross throwing-up noises about how disgusting my stump is . . . The others take it in turns, so my wrist and palm are fondled and stroked by teenage female fingers for the first time in my life . . . Even Sally Bundy snuggles up . . . gentle Sally, younger and shyer and not as mouthy as the rest of them. She leans close and whispers so no one else can hear, 'We've missed you this summer. Well, I've missed you anyway . . .'

She turns my hand this way and that to see the finger. She frowns. She glances up and sees the glimmer of hurt and puzzlement in my eyes. And, not thinking about the reaction she'll provoke, she lifts my hand to her lips and kisses it.

The others see her do it. They all hoot. Sally lets go of my hand and covers her face in pretend-shame, grinning at them all through her fingers. I wave the stump in the air, trying to join in the raucousness of the moment without embarrassing Sally any further. Pete's trying to sing, accompanying himself with a couple of chords on his guitar, while Tricia Turton's yelling, 'Hey everyone, Dave's been kissed by a girl! He's not a virgin anymore!'

And Simon yells something funny, over the applause of the crowd as the band in the marquee finish their gig with a rollercoaster rock number. 'Dave's a dark horse! He's had a girlfriend all summer!'

What? Who? Everyone turns to look where he's looking. The crowd's dense, pushing out of the marquee and into the daylight, and the noise is louder than ever. I'm looking too, puzzled by what Simon's said. But when I glance back at him and see he's peering downwards, into the legs and feet of all the people, I feel a sudden squirming of uneasiness in my stomach ...

'Here she is!' he's shouting. 'Here's Daphne!'

And the gull springs out of the crowd. It hops towards me, its wings outspread. It covers the ground in a couple of leaps, scattering people in every direction by the unexpectedness of its appearance. Pete Shaw splutters a mouthful of beer and drops his guitar. Tricia Turton squeals.

'Hey, this is Daphne!' Simon's giggling. 'Dave's been going out with her for weeks! I think they've been sleeping together! Is that right, Dave?'

The dark space squirms in my stomach again. A chilly darkness. The waft of its wings, or the weight of its cold grey beak, or the ice in its pale grey eyes ... The gull beats up and into my face and brings a draft of winter with it, a shiver of wintry wind right through me.

'Oh my God. Get it away from me, will you?' Tricia's squealing. People are staring and shoving out of the way, glancing from the bird to me and back again. 'What's it got on its beak? Is it blood? Oh my god, it's got blood on its beak ...'

And the gull's standing in front of me, as tall and big as it can make itself. It's found me, among hundreds of people.

It hammers at the air with all the might in its wings, as though driving out the heat of the carnival, driving away the last glorious day of the summer and bringing a chill to the afternoon ... the doom of autumn, the threat of winter.

I see the smear of red on its lower jaw, which I put there. No, not blood, but a blob of molten plastic, to make up for the injury I did to the bird. And a length of silvery wire snagged around its foot ...

'All right Daphne, don't be jealous now ...' I bluster. 'Don't worry, everybody. It's all cool!'

I flap my arms at the bird, poke at it with my foot. The crowd dissolves around it. It retreats to the edge of the quay. It's going to spring off the quayside and flutter down to the green-black waters of the river . . . It's made a space for itself, still beating at the air, clacking its new-made beak to the sky. So that we all look up, to see where it's looking.

High, high above the castle . . . no bigger than a speck on the clear blue sky . . . the parent bird is circling and watching.

It all happens in a whoosh and a blur. The black-back drops out of the sky. Aware of a threat to its chick, it comes down so fast and so hard that it barely assumes the shape of a bird at the last moment. Black and white, twisting and altering, a shape-changing thing, it hurtles out of the blue, its shadow a flicker of darkness on the walls of the castle.

The black-back is on us. Not touching with a single feather, but buffeting with its speed and power, it sucks the air away and goes rocketing by. No air to breathe, no sound. For a millisecond there's a vacuum, a shock of nothingness which steals the day, which steals the real world away from me . . .

And then it's gone. And a rude shouting and a spattering handful of gravel fill the vacuum.

Gobby moron. White sulky face and spikey red hair. The kid and maybe two or three of his friends are pelting at the bird—*my* bird—with pebbles or sand. Someone else, an angry adult fuelled with alcohol and memories of a long hot summer scarred by the gulls, hurls a splatter of beer. So the bird beats away, clearing a way through the crowd and past the side of the marquee, while the kids pursue it and sling stones and gravel and empty cans at it.

It's *my* bird! With a piece of *my* plectrum from *my* guitar fused into its beak! Trailing a string from *my* guitar! I go bellowing after it . . .

TWENTY-FOUR

I guess whatever happens next takes less than a minute. Two minutes at most.

No point in labouring or embellishing with dreams and flashbacks. It's not like the stuff we 'did' with Dad— and he's with me all the way now, because I'm inside his clothes and shoes and I can feel him and smell him all around me—a hundred pages for *One Day in the Life of Ivan Denisovich*, or even eighty overblown pages to do *The Old Man and the Sea*, a guy on a fishing trip, I mean how gripping is that?

This is what happened. The gull goes squirming through the crowds and past the marquee and dives for the shelter of the first big dark hole it can see . . . because the kids are hustling after it and throwing bottles and tins and anything else they can lay their sticky little hands on. It flaps up the steps and disappears through the wide-open gates of the Eagle Tower.

A huge black open doorway. It's swallowed by the shadows in the castle, somewhere cooler and quieter than the madness outside. Shoving the kids aside, I run after it. The redheaded urchin is squealing at me, maybe I pushed him too hard and he's taken a tumble on the uneven limestone of the castle steps. But then he's up again and after me, with his barbarian gang, and I feel the spatter of beer or gobbets of their spittle on the back of my neck as I try to keep up with the bird. A moment later, as I adjust my eyes to the gloom, I see the slither of the silvery guitar string and the bird's escaping up a spiral staircase, up and up to try and get further from me and the boys and the noise and all the bluster and fluster and sheer unnecessary busyness of everything going on outside . . .

I'm in the tower behind it.

Time after time I'm close enough to grab for the string. It's only a few feet in front of me as I huff and puff up the steeper and narrower stairs . . . but I miss and miss and graze my hands on the hard cold rock. The bird climbs and climbs, I know exactly how high it climbs and how dark the staircase becomes, how narrow it gets, so I'm almost on my hands and knees and clambering and gasping for breath . . . and the kids are behind me, I can hear their scrabbling feet just yards away, hear the rasp of their breathing, their gasps and giggles and the coarse cruel words in their throats.

A thirteenth-century tower, the stairs winding tighter and darker. A sooty corkscrew up into a pitchy blackness.

Shouts above me . . . Someone else there, a man's cry of surprise and a woman's shriller outburst of horror. The bird wriggles and flaps past their legs, so, whoever they are, they almost fall on top of me as I blunder my way past them too . . . For a terrifying moment, there's a man and woman and a clumsy paraphernalia of camera and cables and microphone, and me and a black-backed gull and five or six persistent children with scabby knees and sharp elbows all shoving in the darkness . . .

Until we force ourselves past and . . . and a minute or maybe two since the gobby moron threw the first hand-ful of gravel on the quayside, the bird's bursting into the bright sunlight at the very top of the Eagle Tower, with me grabbing and missing and grabbing and missing the guitar string it's trailing behind it.

How to describe it? As quick as I can. Mad? It's the mad-dest minute of my life.

The bird springs up and away from me, as though to copy the wondrousness of its parent's plummeting dive and launch itself from the tower. For a splendidly picturesque moment, it's on the eagle. It perches on King Edward's sandstone eagle and strikes a pose, its wings outspread and beating a blur of brilliant sunshine.

I clamber breathlessly out of the black hole of the stairwell. The gull dives into the air.

Not far. The guitar string is snagged on the rusty wires on the weather-beaten eagle.

I lunge across the turret and peer over ... a dizzying height, the crowds far below me, and the red and white stripes of the marquee ... just out of my reach, the gull is dangling upside down, hysterical as a bating falcon.

I reach for it. I try to tug it up to me on the string, but it's taut and cutting on my hand. I'm aware of the camera crew emerging behind me, their hoarse breathing and their clattering with camera and sound boom ... The kids are there too, yanking at my jacket, their hands in my pockets. The space is too small for everyone and all our silliness.

'All Along the Watchtower.' Nice one, Kenny ...

The first unmistakable chords boom from the marquee, and then the swooping attack of Hendrix guitar ... imprinted on my brain by the countless times I've heard it in our house, enough for me to know that Kenny's on stage and conjuring airness from the aura of the long-ago legend.

Airness. The word's in my head as I crane further over the battlements. My left hand is clawing at the eagle ... It's a keen cold pain in the wounded finger, deep in the crushed bone, cold on the ghost of the finger, the space where it's gone into nothing but airness. I lean further out and down, into an empty space.

I tug at the gull. I feel its breath on my face, I smell it. There's a rushing black shadow around me and mighty buffeting of wings on my head ...

Crack. An odd sudden crackling sound behind and above me, and the eagle breaks off.

No matter that it's been there for eight hundred years. No matter the symbolism of conquest and power that King Edward intended. It can't take the weight of me and my bird.

All I remember? Falling.

My own shadow on the wall of the castle. I see myself falling, the outline of my body and my arms and legs rowing and waving, as though I'm a swimmer in airness.

Whoomp! An impact that whoomps all the air out of me. No pain. But my body bursts. The air is sucked out of me in an explosion of red and white stripes. A moment of bouncing, wallowing weightlessness and then the stripes give way beneath me. Another shorter falling, into noise and commotion … This time, when my fall's broken, there's pain and a roaring in my head.

The music judders and stops. A second of silence, and then screaming and shouting. Squeals of feedback from amplifiers. A muffled explosion, a crackle of sparks. A lot of screaming.

I'm lying on something and I can't move. Some kind of wreckage of sharp hard pointy things.

My body, my whole body is hurting, as though I've fallen a hundred feet or more and smashed through the roof of a canvas tent, bounced off a stack of hay bales and crash landed on the sharp, pointy, spikey metallic bits of … I'm lying on the wreckage of a drum-kit. It hurts.

I blink and cough and turn my head a bit. I force myself to roll over and I see Kenny lying on the stage beside me.

'Kenny? You all right?' He's sprawling on top of my guitar. It's a blackened smouldering mess of wood and plastic. Through a fume of lighter fuel, I still catch the rankness of his territorial piss. He's staring at me and mumbling. There's a lot of blood on the right side of his head and it's pooling out. He's muttering to me, the skin of his face all mottled and streaked, spotlit in a sunbeam which falls through the big raggedy hole I've made in the tent.

I peer through the drifting smoke. I struggle to my feet, and, wobbling like a newborn giraffe, put my foot straight through a snare drum so it explodes like a gunshot. I totter a few yards, stumble against a stack of bales, and my legs give way again. Sitting down with a bump, I put my head between my knees and hear myself retching very noisily, barking like a dog.

Ambulance men hurry into the tent. In no time they've arranged Kenny and me onto stretchers and they carry us outside. The crowd watch us as we come out of the marquee and into the ambulance. They don't seem to know what to do, how to react to what's happened. They gather round in a kind of muttering silence ... some of them splutter in the puther of smoke.

I glance at Kenny. He's opened his eyes and he's scanning the skies above the castle, searching the skies with a frown of puzzlement and anxiety on his face. He blinks and blinks, manages to lift both his arms and rub his eyes with his fingers. Then he stares wildly around him ...

The black-back. My bird, my baby bird. It's flapping and fluttering out of the marquee, my poor baby little brown chick, still trailing the guitar string and a chunk of sandstone from King Edward's shattered eagle. Not a big chunk, maybe the size of a potato, a King Edward's. The rest of the eagle, all grand and symbolic and smacking of empire, has disappeared into dust and splinters and smithereens. Fuck the eagle. My poor baby hops across the quayside and flops off the edge. Into the river, I guess.

The ambulance nudges through the crowd, away from

the castle quayside, through the square and out of town, leaving the Bank Holiday carnival behind.

Leaving the summer behind.

We're moving, but it's a nice quiet sensible kind of movement. I'm lying comfortably on my back and feeling that at last the world is a calm quiet and sensible place.

I glance to my left and see that I'm holding Kenny's hand. He's on another bed on the other side of the ambulance and he's staring. Not comfortable and calm like me. He has a look of terror in his eyes. He squeezes my hand very hard. The effort clouds his eyes and forces a trickle of blood from his nose.

He tries to smile, but his mouth forms a snarl of pain and fear. He whispers something. When I frown because I can't make out what he's saying, he tries again. I read his lips, catch the rattle and hiss of his breathing. 'Did you hear me playing?' he says.

'I heard you, Kenny. You were great.' And I mean it. I heard him, as I was falling. For those whirling, tumbling seconds, it was Kenny Phelps I heard, not Jimi Hendrix. I imagined him prowling the stage, mastering the moves and caressing the airy strings with his immaculate fingers. I heard the whoop and swoop of the music, the applause of his fans. I caught the whiff of the lighter fuel and saw the blossoming of flames from my guitar as he knelt and fanned them higher and higher . . .

Until the eagle tore into the marquee like a meteorite and smashed onto his head.

'Hey Dave,' he hisses. More blood from his nose, blood on his teeth. 'Inspiration, hey?'

He smiles at me. Not a snarl, but a smile. He closes his eyes and lets go of my hand.

TWENTY-FIVE

September. The loveliest month of the year, but a month with a terrible curse on it. The curse of back-to-school.

I've been looking at the calendar. It's Friday the 4th, and schools are going to reopen on Monday the 7th. Not for me, of course, but I still feel the ache of melancholy in my belly for the end of summer.

Already, a cooler wind is blowing through the town, along the narrow street outside our house and into our living room. I've got the windows wide open, as if I can't bear to shut them, as if by shutting them I'm tugging the curtains closed on the muddly melodrama of the last few months. The smell of the wind is different. It's the scent of the woods across the river Seiont . . . the beech trees of Coed Elen, and the way that the leaves are falling on the surface of the water and drifting out to the cold sea. It's the smell of autumn.

Me and Pumpkin. We're in the living room, on the first floor of our little house, both preoccupied in our different ways.

She's got a worm. She's scooting across the carpet on her bottom, grinning like crazy with the joy of relieving a terrible itch . . . and leaving a trail of who-knows-what behind her.

I'm sitting on the sofa, still fragile after a couple of nights in hospital for check-ups. My body's bruised and shaken, but nothing's broken. Perched on the edge of the sofa, with a cup of tinned tomato soup on the table beside me, I'm pointing the remote at the TV . . . No, I'm jabbing the remote at the screen, playing and replaying a particular few moments from a TV show.

'Hey Pumpkin, we've got to get something for you, some kind of pills or a powder or something. Right now, at this very moment, a parasite a foot long, maybe a yard long like a slimy blind snake, is squirming in your belly and eating your intestines ... Hey, stop slithering around on your arse and come and watch this ...'

She ignores me. Grinning and panting, she dives behind the sofa.

The camera crew from Cardiff has captured my fall from the castle on film. It's been on national television, on all the news channels. And the film company's made a quick deal with one of those real-life-disaster shows, so I'm pretty famous.

I'm rewinding. No, fast-forwarding, and then rewinding. I'm crap at using the video. At last I find it, my moment of glory immortalised on the silver screen.

'Here we go, here we go ... the bear ... after the bear ...' I lean closer to the television, although I've seen the clip a hundred times already. In a circus ring somewhere, a woman in sequins is coaxing an enormous black bear to stand up in front of her. And then the bear's mauling her, swiping with its paws and biting with its massive head ...

'Here we go, here's me.' And there I am, after the bear disaster. On top of the Eagle Tower of Caernarfon Castle, my back anyway, I'm stretching to touch the sandstone eagle, leaning and stretching and then forcing my way up and over the parapet ... my feet off the floor ... and suddenly a shadow's thrown across the screen ... a huge shadow, blotting the camera, blotting the daylight.

A shout. More shouting. Those horrible kids, skulking in and out of the shot. There's a flurry of movement, and I'm gone. The camera lunges forward and over the battlements, just in time to catch me in free fall ... an extraordinary second of television film, a man falling, me, somehow attached to a lump of limestone and a brown fluttering thing . . . landing with a kind of splash on the roof of a stripy tent . . . disappearing in the big black hole I make with the impact of my own body.

That's it. All over. Already, there's the next real-life disaster. A racing-car, in a ball of flames, is cartwheeling off the track to crush and immolate a crowd of spectators.

'Do you want to see it again? Eh, Pumpkin?' I manage to stop the video and start rewinding. But I don't replay it. I just click on pause. I'm looking at the calendar, the one which usually hangs on the living room wall. I've taken it down and I'm studying it for the first time this year.

An artist has done an illustration for each month. For January, he's caught the excitement of New Year. February has a sweet image of Valentine's Day. Daffodils for March. And so on, through the spring and the summer, with swallows and cuckoos and cricket bats and ice cream and deckchairs. October and November have Halloween and Bonfire Night, and December's got a snowman and robins.

September? Poor old September. The artist must've scratched his head and struggled to come up with something. The loveliest month of the year . . . but he's drawn a school bag, with ink-stained homework sticking out of it.

Back-to-school. The blight of September. If Dad had been alive, he would've marked Monday the 7th with a bright yellow highlighter and been getting ready to return to the chalk-face, as he called it. He's not here anymore, but I've used an old highlighter I rummaged from the rummage drawer in the kitchen to highlight the 7th anyway.

Not school. Kenny's funeral at Bangor crematorium.

Mum's on her way home. The police helped me to get in touch with her, sending emergency messages and faxes to the aid agency and embassies in Addis Ababa and Dar es Salaam . . . don't know if they can contact her in Somalia. Don't know if she'll make it from Mogadishu to Caernarfon for Monday.

I glance up at the frozen television screen, reach towards it and trace a shape with my quivering finger. A shadow, black and huge, blotting the light. The black-back . . . what was it doing, what did it mean to do, when it flew at me and hit me with its wings?

So the carnival is over, the summer is over.

I mooch up Hole in the Wall Street and round the corner of the castle, beneath the Queen's Gate. A herring gull is perched on top of the statue of David Lloyd George: the great man, one arm raised as he makes some fiery speech to Parliament, has white and green shit splattered all over his head. The quayside is deserted. Empty tarmac . . . not a single trace remains of the Bank Holiday party. It's strangely quiet. The gull on the statue, silent and still, is the only gull. Overhead, a grey sky is lowering to the beech trees of Coed Elen. And the river is black, coiling out of the estuary and into the Menai Strait.

The smell of a damp, decaying woodland. A chilly wind from the sea, blowing leaves around my feet. The cold smell of the river.

I stand on the edge of the quay, exactly where I was standing when my bird sprang out of the crowd and surprised my school friends. Closing my eyes, I try to picture what happened just then, when the adult hurtled past. I look up at the castle, to the very highest point, and I marvel at the height of it and the fall I had. The Eagle Tower, but no eagle.

I peer over the quay. Below me, there's the yacht I spattered with beer. The river is slipping by, shallow and clear, icy cold from the mountains of Snowdonia . . . now, smooth and slow as it reaches the coast and empties into the sea. This is where my bird flopped over the edge, with the guitar string and lump of rock attached to its foot. Maybe it's all right. Maybe it landed on the yacht, re-arranged itself somehow and managed to peck away the deadly weight of historic limestone.

There's a sudden rustling movement behind me. Something brushes against my leg. I jump and wheel round.

It's only a sheet of dirty newspaper, blown across the tarmac. For a moment it snags on my trousers. Then it spins away and flaps down to the river, where it spreads itself on the water. 'Boy defies death in castle fall.' I have time to see the headline, before it sinks and disappears.

Yes, it was the third of the stories in the 'plague of gulls' series, in the *Caernarfon & Denbigh Herald* this August: front page, with a photo of me in mid-air, plunging towards the stripy marquee. It was in the national papers too, a brief account of my miraculous escape used as a filler around page eight or nine. What's really amazing, I think, and sad, is the angle of the story: my survival is headline news, Kenny's death an extraordinary coincidence.

Last week's news. Brian would've joked that the secret of my parricide is safe, a perfect crime. It's already at the bottom of the river, with the fallen leaves of a long-ago summer.

It seems like a dream. But when I hold the stump of my left forefinger in the fist of my right hand, when I feel the ache from the coldness of the wind, I know from the hurt in it that the summer's been real. And the gull's gone. I'll never see it again.

TWENTY-SIX

A dull ache? I wouldn't mind a dull ache. I went to the clinic on Saturday morning and saw the same nurse who tweezed the bone splinters out of my stump.

'You might experience a dull aching sensation if you're

out in the cold this winter,' she says. 'It's toughened up on the outside, hasn't it? The skin isn't so tender as it was when the scab came off, is it? But it's still wounded on the inside, the bone is bruised from the trauma of the injury. So it'll ache a bit from time to time . . .'

She goes on and on, a pretty smile and a musical Welsh voice. She gushes at me because I'm famous, and aren't I brave to be hobbling around the town already? I try gamely flirting back at her. I've heard stories—are they true?—that people who lose an arm or a leg still have some kind of feelings where a hand or a foot's been. If you've had your leg amputated, do you sometimes wake up in the night and want to scratch the missing foot? Is it true? Will I experience anything like that?

Midnight. And the ache's woken me up.

No, pretty nurse, it isn't a dull ache. It's a red-hot pulse, throbbing in the tip of the finger, where the nail would've been. And I know you aren't flirting with me, you're smelling me and the bird and the quarry and you know I smell of bird shit and the damage and death the birds have caused this summer . . . I stare into the darkness of my bedroom. My finger's really hurting me. It's the pain I felt on my birthday, when I came home from the hospital and went to bed and woke in the night when the anaesthetic wore off. And now, worse, there's a churning in the pit of my stomach because it's midnight, Sunday night, and Monday the 7th tomorrow.

I roll onto my side and squint at the alarm clock. I can't focus on it. My eyes are blurred from a restless sleep and the dream that the pain's brought me. I only see the ghostly glow of the luminous fingers, the looming black bulk of the wardrobe, a faint grey light at the window over the street and another blur of greyness in the ceiling. I close my eyes again, squeeze them shut, and I lie on my side with my left hand between my legs, trying to smother the aching, the aching . . .

The nurse's face swims in front of me, so nice and smiley, so bright and crisp in her uniform. I'm smiling too, a death-defying hero. The room spins around me, I can feel it turning my stomach, and a confusion of images and noises muddles my brain . . .

A cheery oops! and the bang of the door on my finger. An amazing splatter of blood. Soggy-red envelope. The mouth of the guitar, a round black hole. A fat brown bird snatching and swallowing my scab. A clack-clack-clacking, a flutter and flap in the wheels of a bike. Old lady with fat ankles, tossing gravel into a hole. Little white dog running in sunlight, a shout and a squeal and a crunch of bones. A heavy grey blade and a man split open, wide open. Piss. Hot piss. A rush of darkness, a whoosh of wings, and me falling and falling, and a shadow falling beside me, my father, miming and mocking my fall . . .

Dreams? Memories? A blur of reality? A pulsing pain in a part of me that no longer exists.

I hear a movement in my room.

'Dad?' I whisper, my eyes still shut. 'Dad? Brian? Kenny?'

My bed seems to move, as if something's nudging and shoving at it and trying to get underneath. I hear a creak, like a door swinging open, and when I open one eye the tiniest crack I see my own face, a glimmer of my reflection in the wardrobe mirror.

Something's moving in my room. My face in the mirror is quivering. A vibration in the wardrobe is making the mirror quiver.

I blink into the darkness. With both of my hands I rub at my eyes. My lost finger is still throbbing . . . The ghost, the empty space where there was a finger before it was crushed and torn off, teased into an envelope and eventually discarded. The wardrobe seems to bulge in front of me. A slab of blackness in the shadowy room, it bulges and trembles and vibrates as though it's alive.

As though something's alive inside it.

My waking dreams fall away from me. I swing my legs out of the bed, reach for the door of the wardrobe and open it wide.

The gull erupts from inside it. It's huge and black, lashing at me with its wings and jabbing with its beak. A mad prehistoric-flightless thing, it bursts out of the wardrobe.

I stagger backwards, groggy from a troubled sleep. 'Get away from me! Get away!' My head's swimming, my hand's throbbing. The gull's a shapeless blur, a hissing shadow.

'Get out! Get out!' and it springs up and up towards the skylight window. 'Get out and fuck off, you bastard! You aren't mine, you've never been mine! Fuck off, you stupid crazy bastard get out get out!'

I lunge forward. The pain in my hand, the fear I felt for Pumpkin, the terror I felt for Dad . . . I aim it all at the bird. I beam it like a laser of bright white light onto the creature which has come back to my room.

'Get out get out!' I yell, and the gull flaps up to the window.

It jams there, too bulky and clumsy to manoeuvre itself through. For a moment I catch the gleam of silver, a silvery thread which trails from the bird . . . and then the gull shuffles itself outside.

I crane to the window to see it go. One foot on my bedside table, I push my head and shoulders outside.

'And don't come back! Go on, go on!'

The bird's just a bird again. Not so black. Not even so big. A dumpy brown seagull a few months old, it hops away from me along the top of the wall. It pauses, turning and pecking at the guitar string snagged on its leg, snagged on the ivy.

It beats away from me. One stroke of its wings tears the string from the ivy. But it snags again, caught on a crack in the wall. Again the bird turns and pecks at the string, frees it from the stone and hops away. I can see the string coiled tightly around its leg.

I lower my body back into the room. My stump's throbbing more than ever, and the doom of Sunday night in the dead of night is even heavier on me. Throwing myself back onto the bed, I try to breathe slowly, and I stare around the dark space that was *my* room. I try to reclaim it as *my* space, to shut out the jarring ugly images which forced themselves into my head, which invaded my dreams . . . to close out the presence of the black-back.

But it won't go away. I see it, as clear as daylight, projected onto my eyeballs . . . the gull with the ring-pull on its beak, which I removed . . . the gull with the splintered beak, which I mended . . . and now, an image of the defenceless, flightless bird struggling along the top of the town wall with a guitar string around its leg.

The certainty of death. Somewhere, tonight or tomorrow or the next day, the string will snag and catch and the bird will die. It'll snag on the shoreline, and the gull will drown when the tide comes in. It'll catch on the castle walls or the river bridge, and the gull will dangle and flap like a bundle of rags until it's dead. Or, in great pain, the gull will peck off its own foot and be a feeble cripple until it starves to death.

Certain death.

I lie there muttering, eyes wide open, as though the darkness will take the image away. I say to the empty room, to the presence of the bird which has shared the room with me, 'Why can't you just go away? Can't you go away and leave me alone?' I lie there and reason with myself, that the parent bird's been so fiercely, so murderously protective, that surely it can look after the chick by itself . . .

It doesn't work. I knew it wouldn't work.

So I heave myself off the bed. In the wardrobe mirror I see an eighteen-year-old youth in T-shirt and shorts, with

tousled hair and an oddly mixed-up expression of bewilderment and determination. I tread onto the bedside table
and shove my head and shoulders out of the skylight again.
A heave, a strong grip on the rough limestone of the medieval wall, and I wrestle myself through and out.

TWENTY-SEVEN

I'm on the old town wall, at midnight, in pursuit of the
black-back.

I remember meaning to do this, sometime . . . didn't I
say I'd go out in the night and see where the bird goes? But
now I'm torn. Half of me wants to drive the gull into the
darkness and get rid of it forever. The other half needs, yes
needs, to catch it and remove the string from its leg.

A dangerous place. Until a few years ago, tourists
walked the whole length of the wall around the medieval
township. But there was an accident: an elderly American
slipped off and broke her hip. Closed to the public, the
thirteenth-century walls of old Caernarfon are overgrown
with ivy, a tangle of roots over treacherously crumbling
limestone.

The gull's somewhere ahead of me. I move slowly after
it.

No moon. A moonless, starless sky. No rain for weeks,
but a sudden flicker of lightning, like a word scrawled
onto the darkness and immediately rubbed out. Miles
away, beyond Snowdonia, there's a grumble of thunder: a
dry muttering, an ill-tempered old man trying and trying,
without success, to clear his throat. Another scribble of
lightning.

So dark. The only thing the lightning lights is the guitar
string. I tiptoe after it. It's a thread of silver in the darkness,
drawing me after it, teasing me, now so close that I bend

very slowly, holding my breath, I feel and miss, and then it slithers away, disappearing in a mass of ivy. I can hear the bird, the beat of its wings and the slap of its feet, and I can just make out the bulk of a clumsy shapeless brown creature blundering along in front of me. But I can't quite catch hold of the string.

And the big bird comes down. I knew it would. I've been dreading it.

But this time it's different. Somehow it's a warm, encouraging presence, not a threat. A piece of invisible darkness, it wafts around me as though guiding me to stop or wait or fumble more carefully forwards. Without touching me, it strokes the space around me with all the power in its wings. The darkness is alive. The gull is a living piece of it.

Quite slowly and calmly, as though they and I are the only creatures awake and alive in the whole world, the invisible black-back and its bumbling chick guide me past all the places I know from Kenny's tour ... conjuring the stories I discounted and the ghosts I pooh-poohed.

Along the wall to the morgue. There's a crackle of lightning, a growl of thunder. I crane over the roof, and for a split second I can see through the windows, the children who slip off their slabs and press their faces to the glass and fog it with their breath. Cold, so cold, the deadliness of their breath ...

To the corner of the wall, where the yard of St Mary's Church is a yawning black hole. There's a shudder of ice, a whisper from far out at sea, and I look down the alley by the Black Boy ... a flutter of rags on a skeletal body, and a figure running, running for the rest of her poor starved life from her starving hounds.

To the Bell Tower, where the gull brushes the bell with its wings or frails the silvery string across it, because it tolls a single chime for a man drowning in freezing black water ...

The past is a cold place. Not a summer of beer and ice cream. But a deadly winter.

They appear to me and disappear, these ghosts ... bogus, or breathed into life by the soft movement of the darkness around me. I pause on top of the wall and stare ahead of me, where I think the baby bird might be. The town is silent. From my vantage point I can see the looming bulk of the castle and the mighty blocks of its towers, and over to my left the streetlamps in the square. No people, no cars, not a dog or a cat or even a rat to rummage a dustbin: the first Sunday night in September, and the breath of autumn lies like a pall.

But I'm not alone. Call them ghosts, if you like ... but they're here, the people who've been and gone, who've been a big or a small part of my life and have gone away and left me.

Dad? Is that you? I can feel you move past me, the warmth of your body. I catch the smell of your breath and your clothes.

Nellie? Is it the swish of a black-back's wing, or are you creeping beside me on the town wall, now, on this Sunday dead-of-night, and leaving a waft of your old lady's lavender?

Brian? Are you here? Is that the whiff of your cologne and the gleam of your silvery crew cut as you go edging by?

Kenny? Hey, Kenny, I got your boozy sweaty scent, whatya doing out here, in the middle of the night, mooching on the wall when you should be snoring off the beers and rum of an evening in the pub?

You're all here, with me, in the warm shadows.

And at last to Porth yr Aur, the gatehouse overlooking the river estuary. Giddy, a bit out of breath, I slip on the matted ivy and fall to my knees. I pause there, gasping, and in a gleam of light from the water below me, I can see that the young gull is tantalisingly close. It's stopped, as though waiting for me to get up and follow it. The string lies near my hand.

The parent bird floats up and away, folding into the space above my head. I can see it, now black, now white, against the sky. It's brought me to the chick and now it's waiting overhead, to see what I'll do.

I feel for the string. I have it. Calm and steady and doing what I know is right, I wind it round my right fist and draw the bird in. It wriggles a bit, instinctively countering the pressure against it, trying to match my weight with its own. But I reel it in.

I reel it in, so so calmly and gently, until I can smell the bird close to me. I love it. Its breath. The warm brown sea-smell of its plumage. The warm salt-smell of the beach and the sun-dried weed on it. It turns its face to mine and breathes on me, as though it would kiss me, as though it might stroke my lips with the tip of its beak and touch my tongue with its own. I love it.

I pull the bird to my body and hold it firmly in the crook of my arm. Easy. It doesn't struggle or flap. It leans into me like a lover.

The night is still and quiet and warm. Just the two of us on the old town wall, with the gleam of the river below us. And somewhere in the dark summer sky, our shadowy chaperone.

Nothing to distract us from one another. Not a sound or a light in the sleeping town. So the bird is calm and still and I can feel with my left hand to the place where the guitar string is pulled tightly around the bird's foot . . .

Yes I can feel it, a knot so tight it must be squeezing the blood like a tourniquet. But I can't see anything. My left hand is clumsy, and for the first time—yes really, apart from my disability with the guitar—for the first time I mutter and curse for the loss of my finger, for something I really need to do and I can't. My stump gets in the way. With my thumb and my middle finger I just can't get at the knot and pick at it and loosen it.

The gull senses my fidgety frustration. It starts to fidget too. It unfolds one wing from under my arm and rows it into my face, slowly at first and then faster and faster and scrabbling to try and get free. I squeeze harder, maybe too hard, and I try again and again into the invisible blackness beneath its belly where the wire's cutting sharply and keenly into the bird's flesh.

Hopeless. Useless. Without my forefinger, my left hand is useless. I'm a cripple.

There's a light. Headlights ... they swing through the darkness behind me, soft and beautiful, slow and gentle, brushing the shadows on the towers and walls of the castle ... a car, probably a taxi, very late, pulling into the square and stopping. In the quietness, as the gull pants more quickly and I feel its pain in the urgency of its breathing, I hear the purr of the engine, the slam of a door, and see the lights arcing around as it turns and drives out of the square again.

The gull starts to panic. It frees its other wing and beats away from me. The worst thing happens ... but what else can I do except just let it go again, trailing the deadly string? I keep hold, and the bird twangs to the end of it, snapping it tight in an even more excruciating knot on its foot, and it flails away from me ... over the edge of the wall.

There it hangs, beside the gibbet. Upside down, mad with pain, a big brown helpless creature squalling and croaking and battering with all the failing strength in its wings.

Pull it back up again? Exert more and more pressure on the knot? No, I lean over the wall and down as far as I can, thinking to lower the bird to the pavement and drop it, to let it drop gently and lose it again, to let it crawl into the shadows and curl up and die without me meddling so stupidly so clumsily so well-meaningly stupidly ...

Footsteps. A voice. A cry of astonishment as someone turns the corner under Porth yr Aur.

There's someone below me, bulked up with a ruck-sack—the passenger from the taxi?—staring up at the nightmarish commotion, at the bird and at me, my figure silhouetted against the sky.

'Who's there?' It's a woman's voice, trying to sound brave but quivering with fear. 'What's happening?' A pause, and then, 'David? Is that you? What on earth . . . ?'

'Mum?'

I go faint, leaning over her, and my mind goes blank. It's so enfeebling that the weight of the gull on the end of the string, no more than a raggedy bag of bones and feathers, wants to tug me over the brink.

For a pitch-black second my body's loose and limp in the yawning space. I reach out instinctively for something, for anything to catch onto. And my hand bangs on a timber jutting from under the gatehouse. With all my strength I grab it and hold on, clenching my fingers on the wood.

Hanging. Twenty feet above the cobblestones, beneath the gatehouse of Porth yr Aur. My left hand grips the timber. The guitar string dangles from my other fist, with the gull flailing on the end of it.

I swing in the air, I feel my hand slipping, I try to dig my nails into the wood but it's smooth . . . rubbed smooth by the hangman's rope.

'David, come on, I've got you . . . I'll break your fall . . .'

My hand comes off the gibbet. There's a short sudden drop and a bouncing impact, my hip colliding with her rucksack as she turns and angles it up towards me. Then a bruising bump as we collapse together on the cobbles.

The three of us. I'm winded by the shock of my fall, but we struggle to our feet and limp from the shadows of the gatehouse, onto the quayside where a little light glimmers on the river.

My left shoulder's burning, as though my arm's been wrenched from its socket. When I squeeze my hand into a fist, I feel a mess of blood on my stump.

And the gull ... it's yanking so madly that the wire's cutting into my other hand.

'Mum, help me, will you? I can't ...'

She sees the bird and the string and she meets my eyes with an impossible mixture of relief and disbelief in her eyes. She wriggles the rucksack off her back and drops it. Without speaking, she takes hold of the string, unwinds it from my hand, and reels it in. She immediately appraises what's happening. Unflinching, as the gull tries to bang at her hands with its beak, she folds it into a neat brown bundle, wraps it against her body, pinions its wings, and tucks it under her arm. From there it pants and hisses and jabs at the air, but it's a prisoner.

It becomes calm. It looks up at her in just the same way I'm looking at her.

'Don't tell me what's going on, David,' she says. 'Right now I can see what needs doing. After all the things I've handled in the past couple of months, this'll be easy.'

She nods towards her rucksack. She sits on the bench overlooking the estuary—the spot where the two old ladies were sitting when this very same gull was skulking around their feet—while I undo the bag and find what she wants. I hand her the silvery tweezers, and she teases at the knotted wire. I hand her the stainless steel clippers, and she snips. It takes a few seconds.

The bird nuzzles at my stump.

It's the gentlest of kisses: the redness of the homemade spot on its lower mandible on the wet redness of my blood. In its tenderness I feel the relief of the pain as the string comes off. I untangle it carefully from the wounded leg.

I take the gull from under Mum's arm. It's oddly still. It knows my touch, the strength and the weakness of my fingers, as I know the warmth of its body and the marvellous sea-smell of its breath. My bird.

There's a flicker of lightning. Far away, in another country, a rumble of thunder.

Slowly I relax my grip. The bird sits on the palms of my hands and lets its wings dangle, as though they're broken, useless things. It stares into the darkness over my head, where the parent bird sweeps this way and that, invisible, a relentless rhythm to remind us of its presence. And slowly, in time with the beat, the young gull starts to stir its wings, stronger and stronger, until it's standing on my hands and rowing at the air, feeling for a grip on it.

It lifts off. I feel its weight fall off me. And it glides away, a long swooping downward glide ... a flap and a flap ... and a longer glide.

It swoops to the estuary, as though it'll crash-land on the water. But then, in the faintest of light which still burns in my vision from the distant storm, I see how it patters the surface with its feet ... beats harder ... claws at the air and launches itself up and up. Until it's gone.

They're both gone. There's an empty silence in the dark sky.

A very long silence. The only sound I can hear is my mum's breathing. At last she says, 'I've been travelling a long way, a long time.'

I pick up her rucksack and sling it onto my shoulder. At the same time I bend to the gleam of the guitar string on the bench, coil it tightly and stuff it into my pocket. Mum takes hold of my left hand, which is sticky with blood, and her fingers instinctively feel for the space where a piece of her son is missing.

'We can talk about all of this later,' she says. 'There's a lot to talk about. Take me home.'

TWENTY-EIGHT

A week later. Five o'clock. A September Sunday afternoon.

The rain's come. I've closed the windows, the first time for months, because a chilly wind's blowing a spatter of spray off the rooftops and into my bedroom. It's already a bit darker out in the street. The season has changed. Autumn is feeling wintry.

Gloomy? Dismal? Not at all.

Simon Reece, his eyes closed, his hair flopping over his face, is sitting on the floor with his back to my wardrobe. He's playing the blues, bending the strings on his guitar until it sings. Pete Shaw's holding down the bass-line on his charity shop guitar. And me, I'm perched on the edge of my bed, strumming the chords on my own guitar—an easy E major, an easy A major, straining to do a difficult B.

The blues, chugging along, the best cure for a wet Sunday afternoon.

Dad helped me to put the strings back on my guitar. Left-handed. Funny, it only took a couple of days to force my fingers into shape and learn three chords, just three, the chords you need for a twelve-bar blues. Dad? Yes, he sat with me, up in my room, in the late afternoons and evenings of his first week back at school, until I pinned down those stubborn, unfamiliar shapes with my right hand and started to strum with my left. At first I strummed with the ball of my thumb, but it was a dull woolly sound I made. A plectrum? my dad said . . . you got a plectrum? . . . and I let him rummage in my drawer rather than tell him what I did with it and where it's gone. He fumbled through the odds and ends that a teenage boy keeps in a bedside drawer, and

154

then . . . hey, you could try with this? . . . and he tossed me a silvery, shiny thing.

So here I am, a few afternoons later, happier than I've been for months.

Tricia Turton's here too, sitting on the floor between Simon and Dave. She winks at me, and I suddenly like her more than I ever liked her before. Better still, Sally Bundy's curled up on my bed, beside me. At first she props herself onto my pillow, but then she relaxes and kind of snuggles down . . . her eyes half-closed, a mysterious smile on her lips, and her hair's just moving a bit as she breathes with the rhythm of our music.

I look at myself in the wardrobe mirror. David Kewish. Pretty cool, a bluesman with a girlfriend, strumming his guitar with an aluminium ring-pull from a tin of beer.

Coffee's coming up the stairs. The warm, welcome smell of coffee and hot toast, and the blues chugs to a halt, just as the door handle turns.

Pumpkin comes rollicking in, leaping onto my bed and making Sally squeal.

The coffee and toast come in, passed around on a big tray. Sally sits up—no choice really, because Pumpkin's all over her—and we make a space between us on the bed.

'Here, Mum,' I say. 'Sit down here.'

She sits next to me and catches my eye in the mirror, sees that I'm looking at her reflection. Her smile, her dimples, the swing of her hair, everything about her—the fact that she's here, sitting on my bed with me and Sally Bundy—makes me giddy with happiness. She's so beautiful, my mum, and so warm. She smells better than toast.

'Go on,' she says, as we sip at our mugs of coffee. 'Play a bit more. I mean, when you've had a break.'

The others are shy. Tricia, usually so saucy with teachers and grown-ups, ducks her head to her plate of toast. Pete studiously retunes his guitar, with a professional frown on his face. Sally pretends that playing with Pumpkin is the most urgent thing in her life, rubbing the puppy's tummy and blowing in her ears.

No, none of this is really happening. Mum takes my left hand in both her hands. I'm still holding the ring-pull between my thumb and middle finger. She lifts my hand towards her, inspects my damaged forefinger and then kisses it very gently. She looks me straight in the eyes, and I can see a shimmer of tears. She blinks twice, sniffs, and kisses my finger again.

'Dad would've loved to have heard you playing,' she whispers. 'It's marvellous.' The others look up as she speaks, so she turns to them and says more loudly, 'It sounds so good, he would've loved it . . .'

No. This isn't real. Simon glances at me, and I can see a little twist of mischief on his face, the twist of a smile on his mouth. 'Dad? You mean Mr Kewish? Haven't seen him for a while.' Then, taking the piss, he says, 'Or do you mean Kenny? Where is Kenny? Is he *working?*'

I hear the quotation marks in his voice. I glare at him. The room spins and blurs and suddenly they're all laughing at me, Simon and Pete and Tricia and even my sweet Sally Bundy, smothering their laughter into silly schoolgirl giggling. What's so funny? Surely they remember that Mr Kewish was diagnosed with terminal colour-blindness last summer and drove himself into the quarry? Surely they know that Kenny Phelps was burnt to cinders at the crem last week with 'Stairway to Heaven' blasting out of the speakers?

No. No no. This isn't happening. The room stops spinning, my mum is squeezing my finger very hard, and our faces are framed together in the mirror.

No. It would've been nice, coffee and toast and playing the guitar with friends. But there's no one. Just me and Mum and Pumpkin.

It's dark outside. An autumn evening is gathered in shadows in Hole in the Wall Street. No friends. No Dad. Not even Kenny. Mum's come back, but the others have all fucked off and left me.

I feel a sudden shiver in my bones and an ache in my finger. Mum looks at me uneasily and says, 'Are you all right, David. Are you all right?'

I don't know if I'm all right or not. A chilly wind blows around the towers of the castle. Beech leaves, torn off the trees in Coed Elen, whirl past the windows. I hear a spatter of raindrops on the ivy-covered walls outside my bedroom.

TWENTY-NINE

'The main character in a story should be likable, appealing in some kind of way,' Dad used to tell our class. 'The reader should be on his side, should want him to achieve his goals.'

He used to talk about endings too, the resolution, tying up the loose ends. And now the autumn's blurring into winter. The daylight fades fast in the afternoons. The wind moans at night. It makes me feel that the summer was a kind of dream, a long-ago dream.

Now I remember . . . I could see it on Dad's face, in the weeks before he died, before he told me he was dying: a kind of puzzlement, as though something had happened which he couldn't quite understand. I remember he had a crumpled, bewildered look. I didn't know what was happening to him, or what would happen. But, coming home in the afternoons, driving me home after school, he somehow looked grey and pinched, his body hunched inside his jacket. He would step indoors from the narrow street . . . and even in those summery days, he'd bring a shudder of cold with him.

My finger aches. Not real, not the real piece of me which was squashed in a door and torn off. But a ghost. Something I had which has gone forever. The ache of something lost.

Summer's a long-ago story. Sounds and sensations and incidents, wrapped up in a jumble of memories. Goals? Loose ends? A few of those. And memories come back, when you don't expect them.

A winter's night. November. I wake up with a terrible shock. So sudden, sitting up in my bed and staring into the darkness, that I might've been grabbed by the hair and wrenched awake.

Freezing cold. The window overlooking the street's blown wide open. It's swinging on its hinges, creaking and bang-bang-banging against the wall. An icy wind's funnelling into the room.

'Mum? Dad? Kenny?' My voice is very small in the dead of night.

Afraid, not sure why I'm afraid, I slip out of bed and cross the room. So cold, in my shorts and T-shirt and bare feet, as the wind whispers around me. I start to close the window.

There's a sound, from outside in the street. Something, or someone, is knocking on the door.

I lean out, although I'm shuddering with cold. I lean out as far as I can. A faint knocking, a tap-tap-tapping, as though someone's tapping on the door with a coin or a key or a pebble . . .

But there's no one. The street's deserted. The town's asleep. I go down the stairs, through the living room and down again to the ground floor.

Tap-tap-tap. I pause at the door, take a breath and turn the handle, open it wide.

No one. Nothing.

I look up and down the street. The wall and its covering of ivy bulge over me. The Bell Tower is dark and silent. The castle is a huge black thing, blacker than the night which folds around it.

I step outside and look up at the sky. No stars. There's a half-moon smothered in cloud. Barefoot on the cobbles, I turn and turn and crane up and up, staring for any kind of movement, until my neck's aching . . .

Nothing. Not a sound. I'm the only soul awake in the old town.

I kneel to the bottom of the door. A faint red stain. I touch it with the forefinger of my left hand.

'David?'

I spin around. A looming shape . . . someone, a long black shadow in the long black tunnel of the street.

'David? What are you doing?'

She moves towards me. She glances behind her and holds her breath as though listening for a movement. When she speaks there's a silvery mist on her lips. 'Something woke me . . .'

I stand up and she puts her arms around me and hugs me. I can smell the cold night air in her hair and feel the warmth of her body. 'Hey Mum, what're you doing out here?'

She looks queerly over my shoulder, expecting to see someone or something there. 'I thought I heard . . . I thought I heard someone knocking. What about you?'

'I heard something too. I don't know. Maybe I was dreaming.'

We go into the house and upstairs together. She opens the door to her bedroom, the room she shared with Dad, the room she shared with Kenny.

'Try to sleep,' she says very softly. 'Don't dream. Just sleep.'

I start up the stairs to my room. When I turn and look down, she's still standing there. She looks up at me, and I see a strange bewilderment in her eyes. More than bewilderment, more than anxiety. I think it's fear.

She disappears into her room. I go into mine. I make sure the window is tightly closed and I slip back into bed. I shut my eyes and listen for a sound in the street outside.

But there's nothing. No tapping. Only the wind.

So. It's November and I've been sleeping in the caravan in the quarry.

I wake up aching from the dampness of the bed. I lie on my back and stare at the ceiling.

An icy silence. Not a sound.

Mum asked if I'm all right. I think I am, I think I will be. Now she's come home, people don't look at me so queerly. It's winter in town, and the quietness is calm and cold. The gulls have left the castle and the old walls, gone to the cliffs at South Stack or the dunes at Newborough Warren. And up here, into the mountains.

Mum is back, but I still come to the quarry sometimes, to the caravan which Brian was making so nice with his books and radio and wildflowers. Not so nice now. The pages of his dictionary are stuck together. The radio is dead. I've put a tangle of ivy in the vase, that's all.

But I'm all right. Mum suggested I sell the quarry, have my own money, go travelling, or go to college. Go somewhere, do something...

If only I could. I can't think about leaving, while Dad is still in the pool.

Tap-tap-tapping. The first and only sound of the morning.

I creak out of bed and stand up and stretch. Only eighteen, but I'm aching like an old man. I open the door and I know what

I'll find . . . and there it is, my bird, tapping at the door with its iron-grey beak.

Bigger now and heavier. An immature bird, but unmistakably different, in the weight of its beak and the cold black emptiness of its eyes. Young black-back.

Strange. No other gulls. Not one.

As I stand in the open doorway, expecting the others to come brawling onto the roof and squabbling at me for scraps, there's silence. Not quite a silence . . . a rustling, like a wind moving in the rowan and birch on the side of the quarry. But the trees aren't moving. There's no wind. The few dead leaves which cling to the branches are quite still, not a shiver or a whisper of movement. I look around me and into the sky to find where the sound is coming from.

'So, where are they?' I ask the question very softly, and I can hear the uneasiness in my voice. 'Is it just you this morning? What about all your friends?'

The gull doesn't answer. It never does. It angles its head towards me and fixes me with a cold black eye. It opens its beak, as though to show me the blob of red I stuck there so many months ago and to confirm its identity as my bird, and it makes a little hissing with its long grey tongue. And then it ducks its head and reaches for something from underneath the caravan.

'What you got? What you got for me?'

It tugs and tugs and pulls out a strip of material. About a yard long. Black and slimy, as though it's been in the quarry pool for a long time.

'Show me. Come on, show me.' I bend and take the thing in my fingers and the gull lets go.

It's waterlogged and slick with oil. I stare at it, run it through my fingers to squeeze the water out.

A tie. A faint, faded pattern. A washout of puce and spattered reds and browns.

'Where'd you get it? How did you get it?'

★

I can't breathe. The rustling is suddenly louder, a rushing of wind in my ears, although there's no wind and the leaves in the trees are still. Dropping the tie, I blunder out of the caravan. The gull springs away from me, and it croaks . . . It's an ugly croaking and hopping creature, like a curious mutant or troll from the slime of the pool. It dances ahead of me, cringing horribly, excited to show me something more repulsive than itself. And the rustling is louder and louder, a roaring in my head . . . as I hurry, barefooted, my heart thudding with the horror of what I might find, to the brink of the quarry.

Something is floating on the water.

Hard to see what it might be, because a hundred gulls are on it. Not squabbling, not squalling, but a mass of grey and white feathers rustling together . . .

As I skid to a halt, right on the edge, my bird launches itself off. It spreads its great brown wings and glides down and down into the hole. Its shadow falls on the mob of gulls, and they rustle aside, clearing a space for the coming of the black-back.

It settles among them. It folds its wings. It lifts its head and yells a hoarse triumphant yell which rings and echoes on the walls of the quarry.

And then? It works its beak into the soft and swollen thing which has come to the surface.